TUNA Christmas

JASTON WILLIAMS   JOE SEARS   ED HOWARD

SAMUEL FRENCH, INC.

45 WEST 25TH STREET   NEW YORK 10010
7623 SUNSET BOULEVARD   HOLLYWOOD 90046
LONDON   *TORONTO*

IMPORTANT BILLING AND CREDIT REQUIREMENTS

All producers of A TUNA CHRISTMAS *must* announce the names of the authors and the original produce of the Work. Jaston Williams, Joe Sears and Ed Howard *must* receive billing as sole authors of the Work, and Charles H. Duggan as original producer, in any and all advertising and publicity issued in conjunction with your production hereunder. The billing of the authors and original producer *must* appear in but not be limited to all theatre programs, houseboards, throwaways, circulars, announcements, and whenever and wherever the title of the Work appears. Authors' billing *must* be on a separate line upon which no other matter appears, immediately following the authors' billing. The names of the authors and the original producer *must* be in size, type and prominence at least fifty (50%) percent of the size, type and prominence of the title or the type accorded to the names of the stars, whichever is larger. The billing *must* be in the following form:

(Name of Current Producer)

presents

A TUNA CHRISTMAS

by
JASTON WILLIAMS   JOE SEARS   ED HOWARD

originally produced by
CHARLES H. DUGGAN

A TUNA CHRISTMAS by Jaston Williams, Joe Sears, and Ed Howard opened in New York City on December 15, 1994 at the Booth Theatre. It was produced by Charles H. Duggan and Drew Dennett in association with Greater Tuna Corporation, directed by Ed Howard; set design by Loren Sherman; lighting design by Judy Rasmuson; costume design by Linda Fisher; sound design by Ken Huncovsky. The production State Manager was Peter A. Still; General Manager was Marvin A. Krauss Associates; Company Manager was Carla McQueen.

The Cast was:

JOE SEARS *as*

Thurston Wheelis
Elmer Watkins
Bertha Bumiller
R.R. Snavely
Aunt Pearl Burras
Sheriff Givens
Ike Thompson
Inita Goodwin
Leonard Childers
Phoebe Burkhalter
Joe Bob Lipsey

JASTON WILLIAMS *as*

Arles Struvie
Didi Snavely
Petey Fisk
Jody Bumiller
Charlene Bumiller
Stanley Bumiller
Vera Carp
Dixie Deberry
Helen Bedd
Farley Burkhalter
Garland Poteet

A TUNA CHRISTMAS was originally produced by Charles H. Duggan at the Marines Memorial Theatre in San Francisco in September 1989.

OPENING NIGHT: DECEMBER 15, 1994

BOOTH THEATRE

A Shubert Organization Theatre

Gerald Schoenfeld, *Chairman*   **Bernard B. Jacobs,** *President*
Philip J. Smith, *Exec.Vice President*   **Robert E. Wankel,** *Vice President-Finance*

CHARLES H. DUGGAN and DREW DENNETT
present

JOE SEARS & JASTON WILLIAMS

in

A
TUNA
CHRISTMAS

Written by
JASTON WILLIAMS, JOE SEARS, ED HOWARD

LOREN SHERMAN, *Scenic Design*
LINDA FISHER, *Costume Design*
JUDY RASMUSON, *Lighting Design*
KEN HUNCOVSKY, *Sound Design*
PETER A. STILL, *Production Stage Manager*
JOE MAC, SHYRL PONDER, CARLA McQUEEN, SEAN ASHLEY
Producing Associates
MARVIN A, KRAUSS ASSOCIATES, *General Management*
THE PETE SANDERS GROUP, *Press Representative*

Directed by
ED HOWARD

for

John Henry Faulk

NOTES

While A TUNA CHRISTMAS was written as a sequel to GREATER TUNA, it was crafted to be an autonomous piece, and has been completely successful with audiences who have not seen the former work. Despite having a Yuletide theme, A TUNA CHRISTMAS has proven to be as successful when produced at other times of the year.

Similar to GREATER TUNA, the various locales in A TUNA CHRISTMAS were very simply suggested, sometimes with lighting, other times with the simplest set props. Individual Christmas trees further defined the scenes with decorations that mirrored the idiosyncrasies of the Characters in the play. The only hand props used were directly related to these trees, e.g. tree ornaments; *all other hand props were mimed.*

Country-western Christmas music is suggested for use throughout the play. Producers are cautioned, however, that permission to produce A TUNA CHRISTMAS does not automatically include permission to use music which is still under copyright protection.

In the original production of A TUNA CHRISTMAS, all the denizens of Tuna, Texas, were played by two actors. It is the opinion of the authors that this greatly increases the fun of the show; but it is recognized that individual producers may wish to expand the size of the cast.

ACT I

Scene 1

(On stage are a table, two chairs and an aluminum Christmas tree strung with Christmas lights. Down stage to each side is a radio. The interior light of one radio is lit. We hear upbeat country western Christmas music. As the music ends, stage lights fade to black; in the darkness we hear a TEST TONE from the radio, followed by:)

RADIO: *(Tape)* This is Radio Station OKKK in Tuna, Texas, serving the Greater Tuna area at two hundred and seventy-five watts signing on.

(Lights up to reveal THURSTON WHEELIS and ARLES STRUVIE, two "down home" radio announcers and local celebrities, in the control room of Radio OKKK. On occasion the lights on the aluminum tree pop, crackle and shoot out sparks.)

THURSTON: Merry Christmas, Tuna, this is Thurston Wheelis.
ARLES: And this is Arles Struvie.
THURSTON: And this is the Wheelis ...
ARLES: Struvie Happy Holiday Report.

(A tree light sparks. ARLES empties an imaginary flask into his cup as THURSTON reads from an imaginary news report. [NOTE: All hand props are mimed, with the

9

exception of those specifically listed in the Property, i.e.
those relating to the Christmas trees in the scenes.])

THURSTON: First off in the news we have the finalists in the
OKKK Christmas Yard Display Contest. We've all been
waiting on this one.
    ARLES: We have.
    THURSTON: We have.
    ARLES: We have, we have.

(Another tree light pops. ARLES exits to refill his flask.)

    THURSTON: And leading the competition as usual is the
display at the home of W.H. and Vera Carp. This year the
Carp's yard display is titled "The Christmas Hall of Fame"
and consists of a traditional nativity scene complete with live
sheep. The Holy Family is shaped out of hard plastic and lit
from the inside and is surrounded not only by the wise men
and shepherds, but the crowd also includes Santa Claus, Bing
Crosby, the Grinch who stole Christmas and Natalie Wood.

(ARLES re-enters.)

    ARLES: Mm, mm, mm.
    THURSTON: Still in the running is Didi Snavely with her
gigantic Christmas tree constructed out of aluminum pie pans
and colored flood lights called "Oh, What a Heavenly Light."
    ARLES: You can see it as far off as Dewey County.
    THURSTON: It draws bugs in December.
    ARLES: It does.
    THURSTON: It does.

ARLES: It does, it does.

THURSTON: Oh, the heat it puts out is awful. And still in the thick of the competition is the controversial entry over at the duplex of Inita Goodwin and Helen Bedd. That entry is titled "All I Want for Christmas" and consists of two life-sized cowboy mannequins stuffed inside huge Christmas stockings hanging off the front porch balcony. A lot of folks were upset by that one.

ARLES: Hell, Sheriff Givens tried to arrest Inita and Helen.

THURSTON: He thought he had a double homicide.

ARLES: He did.

THURSTON: He did.

ARLES: He did, he did. Next up, the local chapter of the Smut Snatchers of the New Order is offering a fifty dollar reward and an autographed copy of the Reverend Spikes' new book, *Cleaned-Up Deuteronomy*, for any information leading to the arrest of the infamous Christmas Phantom, who has wreaked havoc in the Greater Tuna area for years. It seems the Phantom struck again last night and loosened all the lights on the community Christmas tree, and just ruined the big moment before Garlinda Crump was to sing "O Holy Night."

THURSTON: She's still not over the hurt.

ARLES: She's not.

THURSTON: She's not.

ARLES: She's not, she's not. So if you have any information about the Phantom, give Vera Carp a call over at the Smut Snatchers of the New Order. She's running the organization until the Reverend Spikes gets out of prison. Next up, on a somber note, the Coweta Baptist Church in conjunction with the Drop Back and Punt Club is conducting a twenty-four hour prayer vigil for Head Football Coach

Raymond Chassey as he tries for the third time to pass the Texas State Teachers' Competency Exam. If he flunks it again this time, he's goin' into politics. So get down there to that Coweta Baptist Church and pray, pray, pray!

THURSTON: *(Crosses to get an empty coffee pot.)* Well, Arles, you never know what you got 'till it's gone.

ARLES: You don't.

THURSTON: You don't.

(THURSTON exits with coffee pot and changes to ELMER.)

ARLES: You don't, you don't. We'll have more on that story as it develops, but right now it's time for the public opinion section of our show, "Tuna Speaks." And today's concerned citizen is none other than Tuna's own Elmer Watkins ... Elmer.

(ELMER WATKINS, a local redneck, enters.)

ELMER: This is Elmer Watkins for Klan 249 inviting you to our annual Christmas family night and skeet shoot. The theme of this year's family night is "The Whitest Christmas Ever" and will consist of fun and education for the whole family. Wear something white and get a free raffle ticket for our door prize, a butane-powered flame thrower. After last year, I must remind all of you about our new rule prohibiting flammable liquids where women and children are present. I feel very personal about this issue. You would, too, it all your eyebrows had been burned off and never grew back. That's why I wear my cap so low. It's embarrassing. This is Elmer Watkins from Klan 249 saying season's greetings.

(ELMER exits and changes to THURSTON.)

ARLES: Thank you, Elmer. And I tell you, folks, it's such a joy to be here in the Greater Tuna area when that Christmas spirit starts to take hold. It is.

(THURSTON enters with the filled coffee pot.)

THURSTON: It is.
ARLES: It is, it is.
THURSTON: I get all choked up inside.
ARLES: You've always been emotional.

(ARLES holds out his coffee cup for THURSTON to fill.)

THURSTON: I have.

(THURSTON returns the coffee pot to its original location and sits back at the table.)

ARLES: He has. Next up, on the local theatrical scene, the much-troubled Tuna Little Theatre production of *A Christmas Carol,* by Charlie Dickens, will go on as scheduled according to artistic director, Joe Bob Lipsey. Joe Bob, as you know, has become a local legend for his innovative staging techniques, which gave us the unforgettable Greek tragedy of *Medea* set in Yazoo City, Mississippi, in which Medea's husband dumps her for a waitress from Cincinnati forcing her to strangle her kids rather than let them grow up with a Yankee step-mother.

THURSTON: That Joe Bob is a creative fellow.

ARLES: He is. *Christmas Carol* will be a traditional staging according to Lipsey who says that all financial contributions will be chipped in to pay for the theatre's over-due electric bill. But city secretary, Dixie Deberry, says if they don't pay up by Christmas Eve they'll be singin' in the dark.

THURSTON: You know what it is, Arles, Dixie's still upset about last year's musical. Joe Bob said she was too old to play Mame.

ARLES: Well, hell, she's older than water.

THURSTON: She is.

ARLES: She is. 'Bout half mean, too. Remember when she cut off the lights at the homecoming game just before half-time?

THURSTON: That poor little twirler had her baton thirty feet up in the air.

ARLES: She did.

THURSTON: She did.

ARLES: She did. Caught her right below the eye. Thurston, you got that farm report?

(ARLES exits to get the world news report and changes to DIDI.)

THURSTON: Oh yeah, it's around here someplace ... *(Searching for the farm report.)* I don't know where the damn thing is! Ronnie?! Well, I hate it when I have to make it up. I know that cantaloupes were higher than a city skirt the other day. There's something we're not supposed to eat. *(HE finds it under his Santa hat.)* Well, hell, here it is! Looks like beef unchanged, pork unstable, chickens uneventful, and there's not a thing on here about sow bellies. So let's just go to a commercial from our sponsor, Didi Snavely, of Didi's Used Weapons. Merry Christmas, Didi!

(DIDI SNAVELY, a middle-aged, slow moving, gruff speaking, chain-smoking owner of a local used weapons store, enters.)

DIDI: And a Holly, Jolly Christmas to you, too, Thurston. This is Didi Snavely asking you, do you know how dangerous it could be in this day and age to ride unarmed in a one-horse open sleigh? Well, lay your fears to rest, 'cause Didi's is stocked to the ceiling this Christmas with weaponry for the home, the car and the workplace. God forbid during this joyous season that anyone listening should become the victim of a Christmas theft. But wouldn't you rather shoot someone than watch them run off with your new toaster? I know I would. So whether it's a stun gun, judo clubs, or just a simple, old-fashioned switchblade, when you come to Didi's, you'll have a Holly, Jolly Christmas and the criminal will have a silent night.

(DIDI exits, mashing her cigarette onto the floor, and changes to ARLES.)

THURSTON: Thank you, Didi. Now folks, if you can't be with your family this Christmas, or if your loved ones are driving you right up the wall, plan to come on down to the OKKK Christmas party and covered dish supper.

(ARLES enters.)

ARLES: You know, I've gone ever' year since Trudy and I got divorced and I've never had a better Christmas.
THURSTON: I kinda miss old Trudy.

ARLES: Oh, me too. I miss Trudy like a rash.

THURSTON: Now, Arles, where's your Christmas spirit?

ARLES: Don't get me goin'. Trudy and I got divorced because of Christmas.

THURSTON: Oh, that's right, I forgot.

ARLES: She wanted a set of Japanese steak knives for Christmas and I got her a heating pad instead.

THURSTON: That's when she poured all that grapefruit juice in the Christmas punch.

ARLES: She sure as hell did. She knew I was allergic to grapefruit juice when she sneaked into the kitchen and poured God knows how much of it into the punch.

THURSTON: I remember it sure made you itch.

ARLES: Itch? Hell, I scratched so hard the doctor made me wear mittens. I still had 'em on in divorce court.

THURSTON: He did.

ARLES: I did. Trudy, if you can hear my voice ... you're too close. *(THEY both laugh.)* You're too close. And from our world news desk ... Christmas violence continues with no end in sight leaving thousands homeless in M ... M ... Hell, I can't even pronounce the name of the place.

THURSTON: Must be way off.

ARLES: Must be. Well, folks, they must be foreigners, so never mind.

THURSTON: Never mind. This is Thurston Wheelis.

ARLES: And this is Arles Struvie saying Happy Holidays!

(The lights fade and a reprise of the opening music swells as THEY exit. Another light on the tree sparks, just as THEY are almost gone. ARLES changes to PETEY and THURSTON changes to BERTHA. The music fades as a

pool of light comes up. PETEY FISK – proprietor, spokesman, and entire membership of the Greater Tuna Humane Society – enters.)

PETEY: This is Petey Fisk speaking to you for the Greater Tuna Humane Society. I would like to encourage each of you looking for Christmas pets not to succumb to that urge to acquire an exotic animal, because after a few weeks, the new wears off and I end up with it. You may think it's cute to teach bar-room language to that mynah bird, but when your fundamentalist relatives come to visit and that bird wakes 'em up at dawn cussin' a blue streak, what do you do? You give it to me. That baby alligator is a family favorite when he's no longer than your finger, but ten months later when he hisses at your sister-in-law and tries to mate with your luggage, what do you do? You give him to me. Exotic pets have mean streaks and I've got the stitches to prove it. Skunks are moody, raccoons are self-centered and wild hogs have a zero success rate as yard pets. So say "no" to that wild animal. If nothing else, it'll cut your doctor bills. As my grandma used to say, you just give nature some space and it won't try to kill ya. This is Petey Fisk speaking to you for the Greater Tuna Humane Society. Thank you.

(PETEY exits and changes to JODY as lights fade and a second reprise of music swells.)

Act I, Scene 2

(The music segues into a country Christmas ballad in the style of Brenda Lee, as the OKKK aluminum Christmas tree

glides off in half light, to be replaced by the tree in the home of the BUMILLER family. It is a scruffy-looking tree strung with inexpensive lights yet to be lit, and no ornaments except a few icicles and a license plate with the name "STANLEY" hanging near the top. Down stage next to the still lit radio is a practical door to the kitchen pantry. The table and chairs remain as before. BERTHA BUMILLER, a middle-aged housewife struggling to have a happy family Christmas, enters and the lights fade up. SHE briefly examines the tree, then crosses to check on some cookies SHE is baking in an imaginary oven. SHE counts the cookies already on the counter, and begins decorating them. The music on the radio is cut off by the voice of LEONARD CHILDERS.)

LEONARD: *(Radio tape.)* This is Leonard Childers speaking to you on Radio Station OKKK, and welcoming you to Leonard's Let-the-Stops-Out Radio Shopping Spree. Remember, if you can't find it on Leonard's, you're too picky. So I encourage all of you to call in and buy something.

(BERTHA hears something in the pantry, turns off the radio and curiously opens the pantry door. An imaginary cat hisses at HER from inside the pantry. [The actor playing BERTHA inconspicuously provides these sound effects.] BERTHA quickly shuts the door, sighs, then re-opens the door. The cat escapes and runs under the table. BERTHA goes after it.)

BERTHA: Kitty, kitty, kitty. Where did you come from, cat? How did you get in this house? What's wrong with you?

(SHE chases the cat upstage.) No! Don't you go up there! Jody!

JODY: *(From offstage.)* What?

BERTHA: Get yourself down here pronto! *(Chasing the cat off, calling after it.)* Oh, no you don't! Get off of that! Jody!

(There is a loud CRASH.)

JODY: What?

BERTHA: *(Re-enters, chasing the cat.)* Get away from that crushed velvet! No, not the tree! Not the tree! *(The tree shakes as the cat climbs it.)* Jody!

(The cat darts back across stage as JODY BUMILLER, BERTHA's pre-teen son, enters running and follows the cat into the pantry.)

JODY: I guess you found the cat.

(BERTHA follows to the pantry door.)

BERTHA: Is that what it is? I want it out of there, now.

JODY: Ah, Mama, she's gonna have babies.

BERTHA: Not here, she's not. And I don't have to ask you where you got it. Only Petey Fisk would dump a pregnant cat on me at Christmas time.

JODY: She doesn't have any place to go, Mama. Petey said all this cat needs is a warm blanket and some straw, just like in the manger.

BERTHA: Jody, I am not playing midwife to some pregnant cat. I have too much to do today. I have a Smut Snatchers meeting at noon, I have a Frito pie to make for the radio station Christmas party, I'm supposed to be at Coach Chassey's prayer vigil, I haven't finished decorating these Christmas cookies, your father hasn't called and Stanley gets off probation tomorrow and the whole town thinks he's the Christmas Phantom.

JODY: I know who the Phantom is.

BERTHA: And when your sister finds out we have a cat she'll have one herself. You know Charlene's allergic to cats!

JODY: Maybe she'll pass out and we won't have to listen to her squawk.

BERTHA: Jody, if she does, I will make you hold her feet up 'till she comes to. That cat is going back to Petey Fisk today. *(BERTHA closes the door and calls to upstairs.)* Charlene Renee, Stanley Gene. Get down here now, or I'm going to put on the Andy Williams album.

(JODY calls from the closed pantry as BERTHA returns to decorate cookies.)

JODY: *(Voice.)* Mama, you promised last year not to play that record again.

BERTHA: Honey, your father promised not to miss another Christmas. Hitler promised to stop after Czechoslovakia. *(The TELEPHONE rings. BERTHA answers. JODY, concealed by the closed door, exits and changes to CHARLENE.)* Hello? ... Merry Christmas, Aunt Pearl. ... No, Hank hasn't called yet. I think he's caught in that snow storm out in Amarillo. ... Well, it's supposed to snow there sometime. ... No, Stanley isn't up yet ... but he oughta be. Alright, I'll send him over, Aunt Pearl, but I don't want him out in the public eye too much today, not with all of this Phantom business going on. Sometimes I wish Stanley would just up and leave this town. Alright, and tell Uncle Henry I'll be by sometime tomorrow with his chocolate-covered cherries. ... No, I don't trust Charlene after last year, I removed the pits myself. ... Yes, I know it's a blessing you knew the Heimlech maneuver. Yes. I love you, too, Aunt Pearl. Goodbye.

(BERTHA hangs up the phone and returns to decorating her cookies. CHARLENE BUMILLER – BERTHA's daughter, overweight with a sour attitude – enters from upstairs. SHE sighs heavily several times, then prepares a cup of coffee. [The actor playing BERTHA makes the sound of the cat again, seemingly coming from the pantry.] BERTHA crosses to the tree; CHARLENE counters, facing upstage to open the refrigerator. [The actor playing CHARLENE provides another cat sound.] Concerned, CHARLENE opens the pantry door to investigate.)

CHARLENE: Oooh. Ooooooh, my God, what is that?

BERTHA: It's a cat that's about to have kittens and when she does she's going to the garage so sit down and eat.

CHARLENE: Oooh, how grodey! After seeing that I'll never eat again.

(CHARLENE closes the door, grabs a cookie and takes her coffee to the table and sits.)

BERTHA: Charlene, don't lie.

CHARLENE: I'm not. *(CHARLENE takes a big bite of*

cookie and talks with her mouth full.) Besides, being Joe Bob's assistant director at the community theatre comes first. Who has time to eat?

BERTHA: Whatever you have to do for Joe Bob can wait. He's never missed a meal for you or anyone else from the looks of things.

CHARLENE: You'd eat, too, if that old Philistine, Dixie Deberry, was threatening to cut off your lights on opening night and you were the most brilliant director who'd ever lived. So don't knock Joe Bob, Mother. He's the only sensitive person in this hole in the road and if he moves back to Lubbock I'll kill myself, so there!

BERTHA: Charlene, Baptists do not kill themselves.

CHARLENE: *(Crossing to counter to add a massive amount of sugar to her coffee.)* I'll start a new trend.

BERTHA: Honey, how's play practice?

CHARLENE: Awful, thanks to you and those goofy old Smut Snatchers. Whoever heard of a dirty word in *Christmas Carol*?

(SHE returns to the table and sits.)

BERTHA: Vera Carp says they're there. Charlene, the Smut Snatchers are here for everyone's protection. Censorship is as American as apple pie, so shut up. And Honey, I want you to stick around the house today. I want to take pictures of the whole family so we can put them on Christmas cards next year – if I can get your daddy home long enough to sit still for one.

CHARLENE: Well, I know what. Next time Daddy passes out drunk in front of the T.V. set, let's just gather around the couch and take a picture of that.

BERTHA: Charlene!

CHARLENE: Wouldn't that be pretty on a Christmas card?

(BERTHA picks up a box of Christmas ornaments from the wings and takes them to the table.)

BERTHA: Charlene, don't make me slap you this near Christmas. Now come over here and help Mama decorate the tree.

(BERTHA sorts through the ornaments, placing a clump of icicles on the table. CHARLENE surveys the tree.)

CHARLENE: Oooh, it's a sick tree. Connie Carp's tree touches the ceiling and has plastic icicles that look like real ice.

BERTHA: Connie Carp's parents have more money than we do. *(CHARLENE tosses the clump of icicles at the tree.)* Charlene, don't throw the icicles! *(BERTHA takes a crude, hand-made angel fashioned from a small Clorox bottle from the ornament box.)* Oh, look, Charlene. Hang up this little angel. Do you remember when you made that?

CHARLENE: Ooooooh. I never made that. You say that every year.

BERTHA: *(Crossing to the tree.)* Well I'm gonna hang it up over here next to Stanley's little license plate. Do you remember when he made this in reform school? I wish you'd help me. It's no fun decorating a Christmas tree by yourself.

(CHARLENE sighs.)

CHARLENE: You know ... You know ... You know, I wonder why Joe Bob has never been married?

BERTHA: Well, Honey, I don't think Joe Bob is the marrying kind.

CHARLENE: Why?

BERTHA: Joe Bob has always been different.

CHARLENE: Well, what is that supposed to mean?

BERTHA: Well it just means he's out of the ordinary.

CHARLENE: You are so cruel.

BERTHA: Now, Honey, you know I like Joe Bob ... Charlene, now come over here and help Mama with the icicles. It'll be fun.

CHARLENE: I don't want to. I can't afford to waste my artistic integrity on that pathetic little shrub.

BERTHA: Charlene, you've got five seconds to get in the Christmas spirit before I hair-lip you!

(BERTHA plops some icicles on the table in front of CHARLENE. SHE grabs them, crossing to the tree and starts throwing them wildly. Icicles end up everywhere; some get in BERTHA's hair.)

CHARLENE: All right, Mother. Happy? Happy? Happy?

BERTHA: Stop throwing the icicles! You get that meanness from your Daddy!

CHARLENE: And speaking of mean, would you please tell Stanley to rinse out the tub when he's through. I get totally grossed out every morning.

(CHARLENE crosses to the counter and prepares coffee and cookies to go.)

BERTHA: You be nice to Stanley. He has a lot on his mind.

CHARLENE: That's impossible.

BERTHA: Today is his last probation hearing. That is a Christmas blessing.

CHARLENE: It would be a Christmas blessing if he was back in jail.

BERTHA: He's nervous enough about doing that part in *A Christmas Carol.*

CHARLENE: I don't know why. He just stands there starin' like he's in a line-up. Everybody knows he's the Phantom. It's just a matter of time before he's back in prison.

(SHE crosses to the table and puts down her cookies and coffee; switches her glasses to her sunglasses taken from her shoulder bag; ties her sweatshirt around her waist; grabs her cookies and coffee and starts to exit.)

BERTHA: He was in reform school, your daddy was in prison.

CHARLENE: It's the same thing.

BERTHA: Charlene, that part he's playing is the last of his community service. I think you need to show your twin brother support.

CHARLENE: It would be a community service if he left town.

BERTHA: Stanley isn't going anywhere.

CHARLENE: That's not what I hear.

BERTHA: And where are you going?

CHARLENE: I don't have to tell you everything.

BERTHA: Fine. You just stay gone all day, young lady, and I'll lock you out with the dogs and you can get Joe Bob Lipsey to feed you!

CHARLENE: Thank you Joan Crawford!

(CHARLENE exits and changes to STANLEY as the TELEPHONE rings. BERTHA answers it.)

BERTHA: Hello. ... Hello, Ike, nice of you to call back. ... Well, you may not want to wish me a Merry Christmas after you hear what I have to say. ... Yeah, yeah, listen, Ike. I want you to have my husband call his home. ... You don't know where he is, huh. Well, Ike, I suggest you finish your Christmas brew and get off your Christmas butt and go find him. ... Oh, I think you'll find him alright, 'cause if you don't the next message I leave will be with your wife, Ida. You remember Ida? And I'm telling her about that red-headed bank teller that you and Leonard and my husband and half the men in this town play poker with in Sand City. Ike, now I'm already mad I had to leave a message at this nasty beer joint you're in. I'm sprayin' this phone down with Lysol when I hang up. And if I don't hear from my husband by this afternoon I'm cashing in his poker ships, and yours. Now you try to have a merry one. *(SHE hangs up the phone.)* I'm a desperate woman. *(SHE calls upstairs.)* Stanley, get down here now!

(BERTHA moves to an imaginary stereo, picks out an imaginary album and plays it; a Christmas song is heard. BERTHA returns to decorate the tree. A short way into the song, STANLEY BUMILLER – CHARLENE's twin brother, an ex-convict and local pariah – staggers downstairs and throws the needle off the record with a SCRATCHING SOUND.)

STANLEY: Damn, Mama, your mean streak sure shows itself at Christmas time, you know that?

(HE pours a cup of coffee.)

BERTHA: It didn't used to. Everyone has called here this morning but your father, so stop complaining. Charlene's bad enough, and Jody is there in the pantry with a mean, pregnant pussy cat that's ready to bingo any minute now. If Santa Claus walked through that door right now I'd set his beard on fire.

STANLEY: Now that is just what we need is a cat. A little, moody, foul-tempered thing with claws that sheds. Hell, we've got that with Charlene.

BERTHA: Stanley, stop slandering your sister.

STANLEY: Actually, a cat's a step up.

BERTHA: Did you get your sister anything for Christmas?

STANLEY: No. They were all out of sheep dip.

(HE crosses to the table and sits. BERTHA gets an imaginary gift and crosses to put it on the table.)

BERTHA: Well, I went ahead and I got her something for you. And Stanley, I hope no one we know is involved in this Christmas Phantom business.

STANLEY: Mama, I've been at play practice every time the Phantom's struck, so just get off. I've got an airtight alibi.

BERTHA: That's what worries me.

STANLEY: Do you know you're just like ever'body else in this town. I'm so nice to people and they just treat me like ...

BERTHA: *(Interrupts HIM.)* Stanley, dammit, don't cuss on

Christmas. And that was real nice of you to hide your Aunt Ruby's new glass eye.

STANLEY: I put it where she could find it.

BERTHA: In the refrigerator.

STANLEY: She shouldn't have left it out on the T.V. I couldn't even watch Soul Train without that eye starin' back at me.

BERTHA: Don't let your daddy catch you watching Soul Train.

STANLEY: That glass eye didn't even match her good one.

BERTHA: She got that eye on discount. She's always been frugal.

STANLEY: She's always been cheap.

BERTHA: Just shut up about that eye before I throw myself off the water tower. Stanley, I don't want to argue with you today. I do enough of that with your father.

(BERTHA crosses to the tree to attempt to repair CHARLENE's damage.)

STANLEY: Why don't you leave him?

BERTHA: I do not want to talk about divorce at Christmas.

STANLEY: He won't even let you play bingo.

BERTHA: Gambling is a sin.

STANLEY: He never takes you to the movies.

BERTHA: They haven't made a good movie since Audie Murphy died.

STANLEY: Did you get that microwave last Christmas? No.

BERTHA: I changed my mind. Your Aunt Ruby got one of those and all her body hair fell off.

STANLEY: Never mind, Mama.

BERTHA: *(Crosses to the table to pick up the imaginary gift to CHARLENE.)* Stanley, let's try to have a decent Christmas. Here, this is your gift for Charlene. It's that new cologne, "Compromise." I want you to wrap it up and put it under the tree.

STANLEY: Aw, great, Mama. What are you thinking? Have you smelled the bathroom?

(BERTHA sits, frustrated, about to cry.)

BERTHA: I can't do anything right.

(STANLEY consoles her.)

STANLEY: Ah, Mama, it's okay. I'll wrap it up. I'll wrap it up. But we oughta tell her it ain't deodorant. She lays it on like a crop duster. *(BERTHA takes a gentle swat at STANLEY; HE laughs, then rubs BERTHA's shoulders.)* What do you want for Christmas, Mama?

BERTHA: Your father here.

(STANLEY stops rubbing and crosses to the counter.)

STANLEY: Well, what's your second choice?

BERTHA: He might show up. *(STANLEY picks at a cookie.)* Don't eat the eyes off those clown cookies. Those're for the M.Y.F.

STANLEY: When did we turn Methodist?

BERTHA: We didn't. I'm just getting some extra spending money. And your Aunt Pearl called this morning. She wants you over there. Something about a bluejay and her banty rooster.

STANLEY: Are they goin' at it again?

(STANLEY opens the refrigerator and starts to drink from the milk carton.)

BERTHA: Don't drink out of the carton! And Stanley, please don't go to your last probation meeting today looking like a zombie. Wear a shirt and tie.

STANLEY: I don't own a tie.

(BERTHA gets out an imaginary Polaroid flash camera, then takes the license plate ornament off the tree.)

BERTHA: Now come on over here.

STANLEY: Why?

BERTHA: Come here. I want you to hold this.

(SHE hands STANLEY the license plate.)

STANLEY: Mama, what for? *(BERTHA quickly takes a picture [actor provides the flash sound effect]; STANLEY is temporarily blinded.)* Damn, Mama! God, I wish you'd warn me before you do that.

(BERTHA waves the photo to dry it, then looks at it.)

BERTHA: Well, at least I'll have one picture of you at Christmas time. *(SHE puts away the camera to its original place.)* Stanley, why don't you stay here for a little while and help me with these icicles?

(STANLEY surveys the clumps of icicles as HE hangs up his ornament.)

STANLEY: Looks like Charlene's already done that. Hell, that tree looks like Baby Jane had a go at it.

BERTHA: Don't you want to be here when we put the star on the tree?

STANLEY: *(As HE exits and changes to VERA.)* Oh, take a picture.

BERTHA: *(Frustrated.)* Take a picture. Take a picture. *(SHE goes to the ornament box.)* What has happened to this family? Christmas used to be so special. Now it's every man for himself. I can't even get my family together for a picture. *(SHE crosses to the tree and starts hanging icicles.)* It's not fair. Well, I guess the good Lord has other plans for us, but I think I deserve a little peace on Earth. *(The TELEPHONE rings, and BERTHA tosses her remaining clump of icicles at the tree. From the opposite side of the stage enters VERA CARP, self-proclaimed pinnacle of Tuna's "high society." SHE rides in, seated in an overstuffed chair with a matching ottoman. BERTHA answers the phone.)* Hello.

VERA: Bertha?

BERTHA: Hello, Vera.

VERA: Bertha, what are we going to do about that Christmas Phantom? He's hit every house on the block but mine.

BERTHA: I don't think about it much, Vera. We don't have a yard display.

VERA: Hang on. *(SHE speaks over the heads of the audience to her maid, Lupe.)* Lupe, darling, hang that on a lower branch. Vajalo, Lupe. Bring it down. Va-ja! *(Back into the phone.)* Are you there?

BERTHA: Yes, Vera.

VERA: Well, I suppose the Phantom can't be your Stanley. He's been at play practice with Virgil, so apparently he has an alibi; but if he does turn out to be the Phantom, I pray they don't throw him in jail 'till after Christmas. You've been through so much already. How do you hold up?

BERTHA: I'm used to it.

VERA: Oh, and about Stanley's probation. I baked him a cake, but if he does mess up before the hearing we'll just freeze it and we'll have it when he gets out of jail.

BERTHA: You've always been thoughtful, Vera.

VERA: Oh, it's nothing. We have those super-ply freezer bags, I can't remember the name. *(VERA calls to Lupe.)* Lupe. Lupe, darling, where are el freezer bags? Por favor. Freezer bags. Free-zer bags. Oh, never mind. *(Back into the phone.)* Lord, sometimes it's a like a scene from *The Miracle Worker* around here. Oh, I just remembered why I called you. I know what's wrong with your Christmas tree.

BERTHA: What?

VERA: Well, put on some coffee. I'll run over and show you.

BERTHA: Vera ...

VERA: Oh, it's no trouble. It's just across the street. I'll be right there.

(VERA hangs up and exits; her chair follows HER off.)

BERTHA: Vera ... *(SHE hangs up.)* Lord, this Christmas if gonna take ten years off me. One child in the pantry with a pregnant cat, another with one foot in jail, and Charlene's in love with a sissy. I wish Joe Bob would go back to Beaumont or Corpus or wherever it is he goes and take his movie posters and his Broadway sound tracks with him. I swear, if I hear "Bali Hai" one more time I'm throwin' Charlene out of the house. And now Vera Carp is coming over to re-decorate my Christmas tree.

VERA: *(From offstage.)* Knock, knock.

BERTHA: Come in, Vera.

(VERA enters and looks out the window on the "fourth wall.")

VERA: Oh, you have such a lovely view of my yard display from here.

BERTHA: Yes, we do.

VERA: *(Seeing BERTHA's tree and covering her mouth in shock.)* Oh! *(SHE circles the tree, surveying it.)* Uh-huh ... Uh-huh ... Uh-huh. I know what's wrong with this tree.

BERTHA: What?

VERA: You need to turn the bad side to the wall.

BERTHA: We did.

VERA: Oh. Well. I know what. I'll give you all our old ornaments to fill in those bare spaces. I gave them all to Lupe, but I'll make her bring them back. She really doesn't appreciate nice things.

(VERA sits. BERTHA pours coffee for VERA then sits.)

BERTHA: Vera, have you completed your dirty word list from *A Christmas Carol?*

VERA: Of course I have. I'm head of the obscene committee, remember?

BERTHA: What's the verdict?

VERA: Well, "merry gentlemen" have to go.

BERTHA: "Merry gentlemen?" Why?

VERA: Bertha, you know those people talk in codes.

BERTHA: Oh, yeah.

VERA: And there has just been a storm of controversy about "round young virgins."

BERTHA: Vera, that's "round yon virgin."

VERA: Oh. Well, too late, they're already out. I'm not comfortable singing about virgins in any case. We'll leave that to the Catholics.

BERTHA: Uh-huh.

VERA: Well, I'm just an overheated downhill wreck about the yard display contest. If we win again we'll retire the trophy.

BERTHA: I know how much that means to you, Vera.

VERA: That trophy is so lovely. It would mean so much to me personally to win fifteen years in a row. *(SHE sees something out the window.)* Hold on. Virgil! *(SHE quickly crosses to the window and opens it.)* Virgil, leave that sheep alone and it won't bite! *(To BERTHA.)* You know, they say sheep aren't aggressive but all three of these in the yard display have bitten Virgil.

BERTHA: Well, I guess they've had enough.

VERA: Well, I know how they feel. *(Returning to her chair.)* I have tried everything to keep him out of that yard display. Barbed wire, bailing wire ... Didi Snavely tried to sell me that stuff they use on the Mexican border, but, Lord, that didn't even slow Lupe down and she's scared of the garage door opener. *(Seeing something, VERA goes to the window again.)* Virgil, don't grab that sheep there. That's why he charges.

BERTHA: Vera, you should have him seen to.

VERA: *(Sitting again.)* Oh, we'll have him sheared and slaughtered by New Years. And as for Virgil, he's off to military school in No Hope, Arizona, and I pray they can do something with him.

BERTHA: Vera, I'm expecting Hank any minute.

VERA: Well, you could just be waiting all day. *(SHE jumps up and crosses to the window again.)* Virgil, stop chucking rocks at the Holy Family, they have just been repainted. Put that down. Drop that gravel. Behave – now. *(SHE crosses back to the table while still looking out the window.)* Well, do you think Dixie Deberry will cut off the lights at the community theatre?

BERTHA: If they don't pay their bill I'm sure she will.

VERA: It would be a shame for them to do all of that work and then have it not happen. And W.H. and I would ordinarily pay the bill but, Lord, times are hard. We could barely afford to buy new cars this year. *(SHE sits, sees something and immediately jumps up again.)* Hang on, he's got the baby! Virgil, put that down, you're going to get shocked. That baby is wired with electricity. Put the baby down now! I don't how he got that out. I paid Julio minimum wage to glue that baby into that manger. Let me ring you later.

(VERA exits and changes to ARLES. BERTHA calls after HER, then crosses to the tree.)

BERTHA: Vera, good luck with the contest. Well, it's just you and me now, little tree. Let's see if we can fix you up. Charlene's just thrown icicles everywhere. *(SHE adjusts some icicles.)* There, that's gotta look a little better. I just hope I can get through this day. *(We hear a DOORBELL, then DOGS BARKING offstage [provided by the actors]. BERTHA goes to answer the door.)* Get back, Woffie. Shut up! Come on in, Arles. I'm sorry, I think that just means he likes you.

(ARLES enters.)

ARLES: Well, hell, if he liked me any better, we'd have to get married. That's a cute little dog you got out there, Bertha.

BERTHA: Well, Chiquita's a little hyper.

ARLES: Oh, I had one just like her when I was a kid – little ping-pong ball head, marble eyes, she shook a lot. We took her on vacation to Yellowstone and a hawk got her the first ten minutes.

BERTHA: Oh, Arles, that's terrible! Would you like a cup of coffee?

ARLES: Well, actually I came by to see Hank. Somebody turned his wallet in at the radio station.

(HE takes out an imaginary wallet and places it on the table.)

BERTHA: Where did they find it?

ARLES: *(Pausing, uncomfortable.)* I can't say as I recall.

BERTHA: Oh, you can tell me, Arles. I'm used to Hank.

ARLES: Well, as I recall it was in a parking lot.

BERTHA: The parking lot of the Starlight Motel, wasn't it?

ARLES: Yeah. As I recall it was. I'm sorry.

BERTHA: Well, I appreciate you bringing it by.

(ARLES starts to leave, stops, then turns back toward BERTHA.)

ARLES: If it makes you feel any better I know just how you feel. Trudy came home one time wearing fruit-of-the-looms. *(THEY both laugh.)* Well, I gotta run. I've got a lot of stuff to do before the party tonight. You come by the party if you feel like it.

BERTHA: I just might do that.

ARLES: Merry Christmas, Bertha.

(ARLES exits and changes to DIDI.)

BERTHA: Merry Christmas to you, too, Arles. *(SHE puts away the ornament box.)* Lord, Christmas used to be so simple. Well, not always. I remember that Christmas Hank was in prison and I was workin' at the Tastee Kreme. Cookin' on Christmas Eve. And that bread man from Odessa begged me to run away with him. He meant it, too. He'd been drinking but I know he meant it. Just where would you be now, Bertha? Well, I wouldn't have my babies and I wouldn't trade that for anything.

(We hear JODY's excited voice from the pantry.)

JODY: *(Voice.)* Mama! Mama!

(BERTHA crosses to the pantry and opens the door.)

BERTHA: Oh no, not now, cat. Please. It's alright, Jody. That's it, Miss Kitty, calm down. Nobody's going to bother you. Jody, reach up there and get that box down, Honey. Hurry, we're going to need it.

*(BERTHA enters the pantry, closing the door behind HER..
SHE exits and changes to R.R. as the lights fade and an
instrumental version of "AWAY IN THE MANGER"
swells.)*

Act I, Scene 3

*("AWAY IN THE MANGER" continues as BERTHA's tree
glides off. It is replaced with a scruffy, pre-fab tree which
is strung with ornaments made out of shell casings, bullets
and other instruments of violence; topping the tree is a
gas mask with a Santa hat. We are in DIDI SNAVELY's
used weapons shop. There is a customer counter, and the
same table and chairs and radio complete the set. Every
time someone enters or leaves the shop from the outside
door, we hear a COWBELL ring offstage. As the music
fades, DIDI SNAVELY enters singing her own version of
a popular Christmas song and the lights fade up. SHE is
smoking an imaginary cigarette and is carrying a box of
tree ornaments of the same type as those already on the
tree. DIDI puts the box on the table and looks around for
her husband.)*

DIDI: *(DIDI sings a popular Christmas carol. In the
middle of a musical phrase, SHE takes a long puff off her
cigarette, then picks up the song at a point as if SHE had
continued singing during the puff. Then SHE calls to her
husband.)* R.R.? R.R., damn you, get in here.

(R.R. SNAVELY, DIDI's child-like, benign husband, enters.)

R.R.: Yeah, Didi. I'm right here.

DIDI: Right here, my rear. What'd you do with those dud grenades? I need a few more to finish trimming that tree.

R.R.: The last time I saw them your Mama was going through them in the powder room.

DIDI: Where?

R.R.: In the powder room.

DIDI: *(Collapsing into her chair in disbelief.)* The powder room! God-damn it R.R., how many times have I warned you about that gun powder?

R.R.: You said they were duds.

DIDI: Poor Mama's confused. She thinks those grenades are pineapples that Dottie and Clyde sent out from California. Well, don't just stand there like a government employee, get in that powder room and find those grenades ... *(R.R. exits and changes to PEARL. DIDI lights up another cigarette.)* God, I'm not even comfortable smoking in there. I live in fear that Mama's gonna walk into the kitchen to fix a fruit salad and blow us all the way to Tierra del Fuego. *(We hear the sound of BULLETS DROPPING offstage where R.R. has just exited.)* Hey! Hey! Hey! Sweep up whatever you spilled in there, R.R. Pathetic. I thought when the sky turned black on my wedding day that it was just Texas weather. Mama swore it was an omen but I wouldn't listen. Well, it's too late now. *(We hear the COWBELL ring, and AUNT PEARL BURRAS – local chicken farmer and matriarch of BERTHA's family – enters.)* C'mon in, Pearl.

PEARL: Merry Christmas, Didi.

DIDI: Pearl, I've been meaning to call you. Why didn't you do a yard display this year?

PEARL: I'm throwin' in the towel, Didi. Vera Carp

wouldn't let go of that trophy if you sprayed her with mustard gas.

DIDI: Well, maybe she will and maybe she won't. That giant Christmas tree of mine out there is gonna be hard to top. But I really thought you had a contender last year with that Christmas at Colonel Sander's.

PEARL: Oh, it took me too long to get all those chickens in their little elf costumes. Now, Didi, I'm here looking for a gun.

DIDI: I thought you had a gun.

PEARL: No, I threw it away after I shot my second husband.

(PEARL picks up an item, examines it, then puts it down.)

DIDI: Was that the sleep-walker?

PEARL: Well, he should have told me that. Didi, I need something to kill bluejays with.

DIDI: Pearl, have I got a gun for you. *(SHE opens a drawer and removes an imaginary gun.)* Now, this here is a Canadian hummingbird derringer. *(Handing it to PEARL.)* It's light, easy to handle, you can keep it in your purse, and it'll blow the fuzz off a gnat's ass at thirty-five yards.

PEARL: I don't know, Didi. Maybe a gun's too loud. My hens won't lay.

(PEARL hands the gun back to DIDI, who returns it to the drawer.)

DIDI: No problem. *(SHE yells over her shoulder.)* R.R., see if we've got any poisoned birdseed in there.

PEARL: Oh, no. Poison's out. I quit using that after I killed Henry's bird dog.

DIDI: Never mind, R.R. But fix me a cup of hot chocolate while you're in there and try not to scald the milk. Pitiful. Well, let me think.

(PEARL opens a drawer.)

PEARL: Oh, Didi! There's snakes in your drawers!

DIDI: Oh, don't worry, Pearl, those snakes are rubber. *(DIDI crosses to the open drawer and takes out a hand full of rubber snakes.)* Hey, now they're great for scarin' off pests. You sprinkle a few of these babies around the yard and those bluejays won't slow down till they hit Oklahoma.

PEARL: I don't know, Didi. I can't be around anything that don't have feet.

DIDI: Some people are funny that way. *(DIDI drops the snakes back into the drawer and kicks it closed.)* You know, I left one of those rubber snakes in my sister's mailbox one time.

PEARL: You know she screamed like white trash at a tent meeting.

DIDI: She sure did. She claimed it sped up her hair loss. But Dottie's hair has always been so thin you could count it.

PEARL: Oh, I've seen better hair on anchovies.

DIDI: ... but back to your bird problem. *(DIDI puts down her cigarette and reaches into yet another drawer to get out a slingshot.)* I guess the only thing left is the old sling shot and ball bearing routine.

PEARL: Oh, yes. And I've got all those marbles I've had at home for years. I got 'em for Bertha's kids when they were little, but Charlene swallowed so many I put 'em away. But I still got 'em.

DIDI: That's smart, Pearl. *(SHE puts the slingshot into a bag.)* One person's clutter can be another person's weapon. My Mama always taught me that.

PEARL: Oh, how is your mama? Is Mimi feeling better? Dixie said she tried to cut off all her hair.

DIDI: Oh, hell, she did. Poor Mama's just goin' down hill every day. She nearly gassed us twice last week. Twice! Tried to fry Rice Krispies the other day. We're lookin' for a home for her now. I tell ya, it just damn near kills me. And this morning she hops outta bed, says she's the Phantom.

PEARL: Oh, you need to find her a home, quick.

DIDI: Ah hell, it gets worse. She says you and Dixie Deberry put her up to it.

(DIDI hands the bag to PEARL.)

PEARL: *(Laughing it off.)* Oh, no!

DIDI: I tell ya, Pearl, the mind is the first thing to go. Let me get her out. She'd love to see ya. Mama?

(DIDI opens the door.)

PEARL: Oh, Didi, don't disturb her.

DIDI: Mama? Mama? Oooh, Mama! Now you're gonna mop that up. *(PEARL exits and changes to R.R.)* Mama, Pearl Burras is here. You remember Pearl, Mama ... Pearl ... Pearl! Ahhh never mind. *(DIDI closes the door, then turns around and sees that PEARL is gone.)* Well, what scared her off? Oh, hell, I'll just put that on her bill. *(DIDI picks up her cigarette, then goes to the ornament box, picks out an ornament and hangs it on the tree. SHE calls offstage.)* R.R.? R.R., did you find them?

R.R.: *(Voice.)* Find what?

DIDI: The grenades, God-damn it. That's what I sent you in there for.

(R.R. enters.)

R.R.: Oh, I forgot. But I found that old "National Geographic" back there that we'd thought ...

(DIDI cuts R.R. off.)

DIDI: Yeah, I'll bet. Useless, God, I'll do it myself. You stay here, look after the customers. Don't cross that line. God, if you were a cat I'd have you fixed.

(DIDI exits and changes to PETEY. R.R. watches HER go, then shuffles over to the Christmas tree to look at the ornaments. The COWBELL rings as PETEY FISK enters. PETEY's finger is bandaged, and Fresno, an imaginary coyote on a leash, drags HIM around the room.)

PETEY: Hey R.R.

R.R.: Hi, Petey. Hi, Fresno. Don't let Didi see Fresno. She shoots coyotes on sight.

PETEY: He's only half coyote and I've nearly turned him into a vegetarian.

R.R.: Well, she shoots vegetarians, too, so watch out.

PETEY: Seen any U.F.O.'s lately?

R.R.: Not any big ones. What happened to your finger?

(PETEY holds up his bandaged finger as Fresno continues to drag HIM about.)

PETEY: Oh, Fresno regressed. I think he was just a little low on protein. I was wondering, do you sell muzzles?

(Fresno lunges toward R.R.)

R.R.: No. Didi says they're a waste of shelf space. Why have a guard dog if he can't bite? She'll be right back.

PETEY: *(As Fresno pulls HIM off.)* I gotta run.

(The COWBELL rings as PETEY exits and changes to DIDI.)

R.R.: Bye, Petey.

(R.R. takes a toy gun and holster from the ornament box and hangs it on the tree. From offstage we hear DIDI.)

DIDI: *(Voice.)* R.R. R.R. God-damn it. I want you to get back into this mace and tear gas department and put everything back into alphabetical order. *(R.R. takes a grenade ornament from the tree and mimes tossing it in DIDI's direction, then mimes an explosion.)* God, this is no way to run a business.

R.R.: I'm right on it, Didi.

(DIDI enters, carrying a single hand grenade ornament.)

DIDI: **And that milk's boiling over.**

R.R.: Uh oh.

(R.R. runs off and changes to SHERIFF.)

DIDI: Mama told me I was marrying the original missing link, but I wouldn't listen. Oh, well. Too late now.

(DIDI crosses to the tree and hangs up the grenade. As SHE does, SHE sings another carol. In the middle of a musical phrase, SHE takes a long puff off her cigarette, then picks up the song at a point as if SHE had continued singing during the puff. She is interrupted by the COWBELL as SHERIFF BUFORD GIVENS – stereo-typical Texas small town sheriff, fat and obnoxious – appears at the counter.)

SHERIFF: Hey, Didi. How you?

DIDI: I was fine 'til just now. Whatever you want, we're out of.

SHERIFF: You should have been a comedian, you know that?

(DIDI sits and smokes.)

DIDI: I'll accept that as a compliment coming from the town joke. Some sheriff. You've been wagging that gun around for years and not one notch on it. You're an example of wasted tax dollars.

SHERIFF: Well, what do you think about this? I'm requisitioning all your bookkeeping records and receipts.

DIDI: Now don't tell me someone went and taught you how to read.

SHERIFF: I'm doing some undercover work trackin' down that Christmas Phantom.

DIDI: I'm not showin' my records to nobody.

SHERIFF: You might as well cooperate, Didi. If you make me come back I'll bring a subpoena.

DIDI: If you think you're gonna come in here and snoop in my bookkeeping, you'd better bring a Chinese dinner for six.

(SHE snuffs out her cigarette.)

SHERIFF: *(Hurt.)* You make it damn hard for me to do my job, Didi.

(The COWBELL rings as SHERIFF exits and changes to IKE. DIDI yells after HIM.)

DIDI: Hey! Hey! You lay a finger on my filing cabinet and you'll scratch your ass with a stump for the rest of your life!

(DIDI starts to pick out an ornament from the box. The COWBELL rings and IKE THOMPSON, a not-too-bright road construction worker, appears at the counter.)

IKE: Hey, Didi, you gotta minute?

DIDI: Maybe. That depends on what you're buying.

IKE: Now, I've been a good customer, you know that.

DIDI: Yeah, the last thing you bought from me was a quarter's worth of b.b.'s for that dim kid of yours.

IKE: He never had any problems 'til he ate all that plant food. Say, Didi, have you seen Hank Bumiller?

DIDI: *(Lighting another cigarette.)* You know, Ike, I was

in such a rush to get to work this morning I didn't even have time to check the gutters.

IKE: That ain't funny, Didi. I just talked to Bertha. I gotta find Hank or it's gonna be a blue Christmas for a whole lot of folks.

DIDI: Boo, hoo, hoo. I repeat, are you here to buy anything?

IKE: I'll be back for that later. Right now I've got to find Hank.

DIDI: Well, Bertha's parking her car across the street right now. Why don't you ask her?

IKE: Adios amigos.

(IKE exits and changes to BERTHA as the COWBELL rings. DIDI calls after HIM.)

DIDI: You'd better find Hank Bumiller or it'll be "vaya con Dios." *(The TELEPHONE rings. DIDI sings another carol while SHE crosses to answer it)* Good King What's-his-name went down .... *(DIDI picks up the phone.)* Didi's Used Weapons. If we can't kill it, it's immortal. ... Hello, Dottie. ... Well, it's usually bad news when you call, Dottie. What's the matter, is your plane late or what? ... What do you mean, you're not comin? ... Well, great. Why? ... Ah, hell. ... Ah, hell ... Ah, hell, he's always had that. ... Well, don't they have anti-fungal creams in California, Dottie? ... Well, you still gotta come get Mama. ... No. No. No, I had her last Christmas. ... I know you took her for Easter, Dottie. She's still got egg dye in her hair and under her nails and God knows where else. We can't even take her to church. ... Oh, yeah? Well, I've got a Christmas wish for you, too, Dottie.

Yeah, well, I hope Santa craps down your chimney. *(DIDI hangs up the phone.)* God, it is hell being a twin.

(The COWBELL rings and BERTHA enters.)

BERTHA: Hi, Didi. Are you busy?

DIDI: Come on in, Pickles, have a cup of coffee. I'm never too busy to chat with you.

(BERTHA crosses to the table and sits; DIDI pours HER a cup of coffee.)

BERTHA: Well, I thought you might be frazzled with the last minute rush.

DIDI: Business is always brisk when the Phantom is on the loose. You be sure to thank Stanley for me.

BERTHA: I hope to God the cops don't catch him.

DIDI: Oh, Sheriff Givens couldn't catch a cold in the Klondike.

(DIDI sits across from BERTHA.)

BERTHA: Well, Didi, I really stopped by to see if you have any burglar alarms left.

DIDI: I sold my last one yesterday. Are you having a problem with prowlers?

BERTHA: No, nothing like that. I just wanted something to wake me up when my worthless husband comes sneaking in late at night.

DIDI: Has Hank been out tom-cattin' again?

BERTHA: I tell you, Didi, it's hard to hold up when the

whole town knows my husband's as useless as ice trays in hell.

DIDI: Don't get me started. R.R.'s been on a wondering binge lately. You know, Bertha, I often wonder how such well brought-up girls like you and me could have married so bad.

BERTHA: It's a mystery.

DIDI: R.R.'s drinking has only gotten worse. He wanders off so much I decided I'd better find out something about safe sex.

BERTHA: *(Flustered.)* Oh, Didi! I swear!

DIDI: Can you imagine how depressed I got when I found out that's what we'd been doin' all along?

BERTHA: Well, I suppose some things are better left unknown.

DIDI: Amen, hallelujah.

BERTHA: Was that Ike Thompson I saw sneakin' away?

DIDI: Yeah. There's another one just as worthless as titties on a boar hog. But back to your Hank problem. I can order that burglar alarm for you.

BERTHA: No, that's alright, Didi. I'll just do what I've always done.

DIDI: What's that?

BERTHA: Rearrange all the furniture and unscrew all the light bulbs.

(BERTHA and DIDI both laugh.)

DIDI: Pickles, Pickles, Pickles. We sure knew what we were doing back in high school when we voted you the class wit.

BERTHA: Sometimes you have to laugh to keep from cryin'. *(BERTHA rises.)* Well, I gotta run. It'll take me a while to move that sofa. *(SHE laughs. DIDI laughs, too.)* Merry Christmas, Didi.

DIDI: Merry Christmas, Bertha. *(We hear the COWBELL as BERTHA exits and changes to PEARL. DIDI calls after HER.)* Don't strain your back.

(DIDI crosses to the radio while SHE sings another carol. In the middle of a musical phrase, SHE takes a long puff off her cigarette, then picks up the song at a point as if SHE had continued singing during the puff. DIDI turns on the radio. The voice of LEONARD CHILDERS comes over the radio.)

LEONARD: *(Radio tape.)* Okay, folks, we're back with Leonard's Let-the-Stops-Out Radio Shopping Spree. Now folks, I haven't sold anything in weeks. I'm so desperate I'll take hot checks. Where's your Christmas spirit? We've got great merchandise here. C'mon now, gimme a call.

(During the above speech, DIDI thinks of something, picks up the phone and dials. SHE turns down the radio.)

DIDI: Leonard? Didi Snavely. No, I didn't call to buy nothin'. I called to talk to you about that egg separator I bought from you last March. It had a ten-month guarantee. ... It broke in nine and a half. ... What do you mean you don't want to talk about it on the air? Well, maybe you'd rather talk about that red-headed bank clerk from Sand City that you go bowling with every other Friday night. ... Yeah, I know your wife could be listening, I hope to God she is. Can you hear me Reba? Reba? Can you hear me? ... Don't talk to me about ruining your Christmas, Leonard. My husband's a drunk who sees flying saucers. My Mama's lost what's left of her mind. My sister, Dottie, had to call up and show her butt. My Christmas has been ruined. I just thought I'd ring you up and ruin yours. *(We hear a CAR speed by.)* Well, I just saw Reba heading your way in her Land Rover. If I were you, Leonard, and I wanted to see New Years in one piece, I'd start dashing through the snow.

(DIDI hangs up the phone. SHE starts to sing another carol as SHE crosses to pick up the box of ornaments. In the middle of a musical phrase, SHE takes a long puff off her cigarette, then picks up the song at a point as if SHE had continued singing during the puff. The lights fade and an instrumental tag of her song swells over DIDI's last phrase as SHE exits and changes to STANLEY.)

Act I, Scene 4

(The setting is the yard of AUNT PEARL BURRAS. DIDI's tree and the counter have gone. We hear the sound of BLUEJAYS all over the theatre as PEARL enters and the lights fade up. Looking annoyed at the imaginary bluejays, SHE puts her purse down on the table and takes out the sling shot. Pulling a chair downstage, SHE sits and takes aim.)

PEARL: Hold still, you little ... long enough for me to get a bead on you.

(PEARL fires and misses, then mouths "dammit." STANLEY enters from behind HER.)

STANLEY: Pearl.

PEARL: Oh, come out, Stanley, sit a spell. I'm out here trying to kill these bluejays.

STANLEY: You don't give up on the bluejays, do you, Pearl?

PEARL: Oh, they're so loud, they've got my banty rooster upset. He's got the hens so nervous, they won't lay. I'm losing egg money hand over fist. Pull up this chair. I want to talk to you.

(STANLEY pulls up the other chair next to PEARL.)

STANLEY: What is it, Pearl?

PEARL: Oh, Stanley, I'm worried. There was a white mule in my dream last night.

STANLEY: That's not a sign of death, is it, Pearl?

PEARL: Oh, no, that's a white horse. A white mule is usually nothing more than car trouble. I'd appreciate it if you'd look under the hood of that Pontiac before you go.

STANLEY: Sure. I'll be glad to. You know who I dreamed about? Remember that weenie dog you had that could spell?

PEARL: Doc, the dash hound. Got him from Petey Fisk. Of course, at the time we didn't know he was a cat-hater.

STANLEY: Ain't never seen anything like it, just say the word cat and he'd go hog wild.

PEARL: It got so bad we couldn't say cat. We started spelling it and he still went crazy.

STANLEY: *(Laughing.)* He could spell cat.

PEARL: *(Laughing.)* Oh, we had a spelling dog.

(THEY both laugh.)

STANLEY: What ever happened to that dog, Pearl?

PEARL: Doc? Mildred Jean Perkins' cat killed him.

STANLEY: No. What was that cat's name?

PEARL: Itty Bitty.

STANLEY: Itty God-damned Bitty. Now, who in the hell would name a cat that size Itty Bitty?

PEARL: That brain-damaged child of theirs, Randy. He wasn't right in the head but they let him name that cat.

STANLEY: How did Itty Bitty kill Doc?

PEARL: Oh, she kinda rolled on her back over there across the street and lured old Doc right under the wheels of a Lone Star beer truck.

STANLEY: Damn, it's a shame to lose a good dog like that, that could spell.

PEARL: You know, Stanley, it's too bad you didn't have your taxidermy license at the time. You could have stuffed ol' Doc for us. Oh, it's the only way to have animals, stuffed and hanging on the wall. All you have to do is dust 'em once a week.

STANLEY: Well, they don't keep you up at night.

PEARL: You're so lucky to have a skill. You should leave Tuna. Folks around here will keep you lookin' back. You need to get out and tackle life, use your gifts, don't be like me and throw away a skill.

STANLEY: I never knew you had a skill, Pearl.

PEARL: Oh, yes, I was a riveter in Houston back during the war.

STANLEY: A riveter?

PEARL: The Japs never sank one of my ships. I put in so much over-time all my fillings just flew out. I had to quit. Stanley, has your daddy come home?

STANLEY: Hell, Pearl, Daddy's never home.

PEARL: You make sure your Mama has a good Christmas.

STANLEY: Yeah. I got her a gift certificate down at the Conoco – five free oil changes.

PEARL: Staying out of trouble is Christmas present enough. What do you want Santy Claus to bring you?

STANLEY: A bus ticket out of this black hole. I don't know, out West would be nice. Your friend, Dixie Deberry ain't making my life any easier.

PEARL: How so?

STANLEY: Oh, she's making a fuss down at the Little Theatre.

PEARL: Oh, how's that goin'?

STANLEY: Shoot. Nobody knows their lines, they're all fightin' like cats in a bag. And Joe Bob's blaming the Phantom, says he's got everybody so upset they can't think. And they're all lookin' at me out of the corner of their eyes. I tell ya Pearl, I've had it up to my ass with this sorry excuse for a town and somebody's going to pay.

PEARL: Oh, Stanley, don't lose your head.

STANLEY: Once I get off probation I'm gonna sneak down to the 4-H barn and spray paint the private parts of all the livestock. Let 'em hang blue ribbons on that.

PEARL: You don't want to do that.

STANLEY: And I've got me a defanged rattlesnake that's gonna wind up in somebody's commode, I just haven't decided whose yet.

PEARL: Well, that'll keep 'em regular.

STANLEY: And Sheriff Givens better stop following me around like a bird dog. Damn, he's determined to catch me doing something.

PEARL: Oh, Buford Givens. He's loopy, always has been. When he was a teenage boy he wet the bed at church camp.

STANLEY: No.

PEARL: Oh, it was terrible. They called him Rubber Sheets.

STANLEY: *(Laughs.)* Rubber Sheets. Rubber Sheets Givens. I like the sound of that. Well, Rubber Sheets ain't gonna catch me doin' diddly. Once this play is over, I'm gonna get even and get the hell out of Dodge.

PEARL: Oh, Stanley, I just had a revelation! If Dixie shuts the lights off on the play, you won't complete your probation. Lord, she has to extend, that's all there is to it. Oh my God, I forgot about the Phantom!

STANLEY: The Phantom?

PEARL: Never you mind. Just get Dixie over here quick.

STANLEY: Hell, Pearl, Dixie ain't gonna listen to me, I'm a felon.

PEARL: Oh, tell her it's a red alert. Now scat.

STANLEY: What the hell ... ?

PEARL: Just go, Stanley, go! *(STANLEY exits and changes to DIXIE. PEARL takes out an imaginary cellular telephone from her purse and dials.)* Hello, Is Sheriff Givens there? ... Put him on. ... Oh, Sheriff, this is Pearl Burras. I want to report a theft. Four of my Rhode Island reds are missing. I got up this morning and they were gone. Oh, do you suppose it was the Phantom? ... You ought to drive by here more often. I'm a taxpayer. Those hens are my livelihood. ... You don't have time? I see. Well, you'd find time if that Phantom stole your rubber sheets! *(SHE laughs and hangs up the phone. We hear BLUEJAYS again.)* Oh, my God, he's back. *(SHE crosses back to get her sling shot and takes aim.)* Stop that hoppin' around. Hold still ...

(DIXIE DEBERRY – Tuna City Secretary, a cantankerous old woman with a black belt in karate – enters.)

DIXIE: Pearl, why'd you send that slobbering hippie over to my house?

PEARL: Oh, Dixie, don't distract me. This marble has that bluejay's name on it. *(SHE fires and misses. [NOTE: Actors must predetermine specific visual locations for the imaginary bluejays.])* Oh, just a nose-hair off.

DIXIE: Now, Pearl, you're going about this all wrong. You've got to think like a bird if you want to kill one. Sing to 'em.

PEARL: I never heard of anybody singing to a bluejay.

DIXIE: You damn sure never killed one neither.

PEARL: Well, I hope they like the Andrews Sisters.

DIXIE: Shhh ... , there he is. Sing, Pearl, sing!

(PEARL starts to sing as SHE loads her sling shot.)

PEARL:
DOWN IN THE MEADOW IN AN ITTY BITTY POOL,
SWAM THREE LITTLE FISHIES AND THE MAMA
    FISHY, TOO.

(DIXIE chimes in.)

BOTH:

SWIM SAID THE MAMA FISHY, SWIM IF YOU CAN,
SO THEY SWAM AND THEY SWAM RIGHT OVER THE
DAM ...

*(PEARL fires and misses. The actors follow the imaginary
bird's flight off left.)*

BOTH: Oooh.

DIXIE: Nearly got him.

PEARL: He'll get the word out.

DIXIE: Maybe you should sing something more
contemporary, Pearl.

PEARL: *(SHE remembers something.)* Dixie!

(DIXIE is startled by PEARL.)

DIXIE: Damn, Pearl, don't scare me like that. My heart's
not strong. I'm older than Alley Oop. I can't take loud noises.

PEARL: Oh, I'm sorry, Dixie, but I just remembered. You
can't shut the lights off on *Christmas Carol.*

DIXIE: Says who?

PEARL: My nephew, Stanley, has to be in that darn-fool
play to finish his probation.

DIXIE: *(Motioning to PEARL.)* Sit down, Pearl.

PEARL: It'll just ruin Christmas for all of us if he doesn't
get off. Rubber Sheets is watching him like a hawk. If he slips
up once he's a goner.

DIXIE: I'd like to help you, Pearl, but I can't. Why if I let
that Little Theatre off their light bill, every light bill in town
would go unpaid ...

PEARL: But ...

DIXIE: That's revenue, Pearl, that's how we pay for stop signs and "do not litter" signs. If that money runs out the traffic'd get snarled and litter would pile up 'til you're just knee-deep in garbage and hot-rodders and then your insurance rates'd go sky-high, sky god-damn high ...

PEARL: I know that ...

DIXIE: Filth and disrespect breed crime, Pearl, which draws gambling and the Mafia and the next thing you know we'll have pari-mutual betting and liquor by the drink, parallel parking on Sundays ...

PEARL: Now, Dixie ...

DIXIE: We won't be able to park for the god-damn whiskey bottles and before you can say scat the Communists will just be pouring across the Rio Grande and that'll be the end of civilization as we know it.

PEARL: But all I'm asking ...

DIXIE: No! No buts, Pearl. If Stanley wants to get off probation he can drag his worthless butt down to the welfare office and lick stamps for me, but I'm not turning my home town over to Fi–del Castro and that is that. Look, Pearl, he's back.

(The imaginary bluejay has returned down stage of the women. As PEARL loads her sling shot, SHE sings.)

PEARL:
DON'T SIT UNDER THE APPLE TREE
WITH ANYONE ELSE BUT ME,
ANYONE ELSE BUT ME ...
(SHE misses again. PEARL and DIXIE turn full circle to

follow the bird's exit off left.) Oh, you dirty bird, you.
    DIXIE: Maybe he'd like some Lionel Ritchie.
    PEARL: *(Once again out of nowhere.)* Oh! Dixie!

(DIXIE is startled as before.)

    DIXIE: Damn, Pearl, you did it again.
    PEARL: Dixie, we're in trouble. We're in big, big trouble. Mimi Bird's been babblin'. She told Didi that the three of us are the Phantom.
    DIXIE: Aaah! She's gotta shut up! She's gotta shut up or we'll all be wearing striped pajamas! This is all your fault, Pearl. I told you Mimi would be the first one to crack. She nearly got us caught in '32.
    PEARL: Now we gotta be calm. You're too damn old to be peering through jail bars.

(PEARL wags her finger at DIXIE.)

    DIXIE: Don't you stick that finger in my face!
    PEARL: Damn you!
    DIXIE: I know karate! I know karate!

(THEY tussle. DIXIE notices something.)

    BOTH: Rubber Sheets!
    PEARL: Rubber Sheets! Sit down, Dixie, quick, sit down! Wave! Wave to him! Wave! *(THEY both quickly sit and give one long wave in unison to the SHERIFF as we hear his CAR pass by.)* We're just out here bein' old ladies. *(After a moment the SHERIFF is gone.)* Lord, I think we're safe. Who's gonna

believe an old woman like Mimi with all that egg dye in her hair?

DIXIE: God, she looks like death chewin' on a cracker.

BOTH: Ohhh ...

DIXIE: But the heat'll be on now. We won't be able to be the Phantom anymore, and that's always been my favorite part of Christmas. I guess our party's over.

PEARL: Our bubble's burst.

DIXIE: It's our last waltz.

PEARL: It's the end of the line.

DIXIE: Adios amigos.

PEARL: Sia nora.

DIXIE: Twenty-two skiddoo.

PEARL: Goodnight, Irene.

(DIXIE starts to sing. PEARL joins in.)

DIXIE:
GOODNIGHT, IRENE,
  BOTH:
GOODNIGHT, IRENE,
I'LL SEE YOU IN ...

(DIXIE sees the imaginary bluejay again directly down stage and jumps up.)

DIXIE: Give me that sling shot. *(PEARL hands the sling shot and a marble to DIXIE, who starts singing "THE YELLOW ROSE OF TEXAS.")*
OH, THERE IS A ROSE IN TEXAS,
THE FINEST EVER GREW.

HER EYES ARE BRIGHT AS DIAMONDS,
THEY SPARKLE LIKE THE DEW.
YOU CAN TALK ABOUT YOUR CLEMENTINE ...
(DIXIE fires on the word "Clementine" and makes a direct hit on the bluejay.) Ha!

PEARL: *(Elated.)* Bingo!

DIXIE: Never knew what hit him.

PEARL: Good shot. Dixie! We'll save him for Stanley and have him stuffed.

DIXIE: Squawk now, loud mouth.

(THEY both laugh and then sigh together. After a moment, PEARL speaks.)

PEARL: You know, Dixie, I've been thinking. It's not like the Christmas Phantom to up and disappear just because one old lady with cake colorin' in her hair and one foot in the grave starts ramblin'.

DIXIE: You know, it might look suspicious at that.

PEARL: Well, if the Phantom is down to his last prank ...

DIXIE: Shhh ...

PEARL: ... I think it ought to be a doozie.

DIXIE: Ohhh. I haven't seen that look in your eye since you snatched the toupee off that faith healer back in Wichita Falls.

PEARL: Oh, he claimed to heal the sick, but he couldn't even grow hair. Now, Dixie, we need to put our thinkin' caps on. Only the best yard will do. *(THEY think for a moment, then look at each other with realization.)* She's had it coming for fifteen years.

(THEY laugh. We hear another BLUEJAY. DIXIE sees it directly down stage.)

Dixie: Shhhh, Pearl, sing.

(PEARL sings as Dixie loads and aims the sling shot while the lights start to fade with the setting sun.)

Pearl:
YOU CAN TALK ABOUT YOUR CLEMENTINE,
AND SING OF ROSALIE,
 Both:
BUT THE YELLOW ROSE OF TEXAS
IS THE ONLY GIRL FOR ME.

(Lights to black. DIXIE changes to HELEN. PEARL changes to INITA.)

END OF ACT ONE

ACT II

Scene 1

(The scene is played in front of the drawn curtain. The setting is the Tuna High School gymnasium. As the audience is settling, we hear the Tuna High School Clawin' Jaguar Band playing a MEDLEY OF CHRISTMAS FAVORITES. Some of the music should sound so bad that the tunes are almost unrecognizable. Near the end of the last number, the house lights fade up on the radio. The music ends with a botched finale and muted applause. On the radio we hear:)

THURSTON: *(Radio tape.)* Merry Christmas, this is Radio Station OKKK broadcasting live from the Tuna High School gymnasium where the social event of the Christmas season is underway.

ARLES: *(Radio tape.)* Yes, folks, in a few minutes we'll all know the winner of the OKKK Christmas Yard Display Contest. And the tension is mounting. It is.

THURSTON: *(Radio tape.)* It is.

ARLES: *(Radio tape.)* It is, it is. Will Vera Carp and family claim fifteen wins in a row in spite of her disastrous experience tonight due to the Christmas Phantom?

THURSTON: *(Radio tape.)* Or will Didi Snavely claim first place despite retina damage to two of the judges?

ARLES: *(Radio tape.)* And we can't count out Helen and Inita whose dark-horse entry could surprise. And now the moment of truth has arrived as Thurston will announce this year's winner.

63

THURSTON: *(Radio tape.)* You'll have to read it, Arles, hell, my hands won't stop shaking.

ARLES: *(Radio tape.)* God almighty, give me that. And the winner of the OKKK Christmas Yard Display Contest and the non-stop weekend in Laredo goes to ... *(We hear the sound of the ENVELOPE OPENING.)* Inita Goodwin and Helen Bedd for "All I Want for Christmas."

(We hear CHEERS AND APPLAUSE. Lights come up on stage and in the house as INITA GOODWIN and HELEN BEDD rush down the aisle of the theatre and up on to the stage. THEY meet center stage, hug each other, obviously beside themselves. THEY wave and blow kisses to the audience.)

HELEN: Oh, thank you! Thank you so much. I just don't know where to start.

INITA: *(Stepping in.)* I do. We want to thank our boy friends who inspired the whole display.

HELEN: That's right. So muchas gracias to Donny and Danny.

INITA: Kenny Ray, Preston and Garland.

HELEN: Duke, Clayton and Duane.

HELEN & INITA: And Randy!

(THEY laugh. INITA looks out to the audience.)

INITA: What's going on over there?

HELEN: It looks to me like Vera Carp has fainted. Isn't that just like her at our big moment?

INITA: Y'all leave her alone. She's gonna be hell to deal with when she comes to.

(HELEN steps forward.)

HELEN: I want to say something now. You know, there are times in life when everything starts to get to you. I know for those of us in the food service business, there are days when the grill is smoking, the ice machine is spittin' cubes at you, and the poppy seeds are falling off the buns, when it's easy to question whether Tuna can offer enough to aspiring career women like us. But then something like this just comes out of the blue. It just encourages me so much, I just want to go back to school and get my G.E.D.

INITA: Well, I'm grateful, I really am, but I'm not going that far.

HELEN: And we want to recognize the other finalists.

INITA: We do. Somebody tell that to Vera when she comes to. Now that that's out of the way, this gal's ready to rock n' roll!

HELEN: Great. So we'll see everybody at the OKKK party later tonight.

INITA: That's right. And if Dixie cuts off the lights on the play, we'll start early. *(INITA looks out to the side of the audience.)* Helen! Is that Sheriff Givens out there puttin' a ticket on your Mitsubishi?

HELEN: It sure is!

INITA: Get away from that truck, Rubber Sheets. *(As SHE exits through the curtain.)* C'mon, Helen, let's get outta here.

HELEN: Hey! You put a ticket on my pick-up truck and I'll slip something in your chili dog next time you come in. *(SHE waves to the audience as SHE exits through the curtain.)* Bye!

(The stage and house lights fade and honky tonk music swells.)

Act II, Scene 2

(The curtain opens to reveal the interior of the Tastee Kreme, Tuna's premiere restaurant. On stage are the same table and chairs. With them is a Christmas tree made out of tumbleweeds and decorated with cowboy and other western-style ornaments. On one side down stage is a walk-up window to the outside. A customer counter is up stage of the table; it leads off stage to the kitchen in the wings. HELEN and INITA enter.)

INITA: Hit the music! I'll turn on the grill.

(HELEN turns on the radio and dances. INITA goes into the kitchen, then returns when the music segues into:)

ARLES: *(Radio tape.)* This is Arles Struvie with an OKKK early evening news quickie. Well, it's all over but the screaming as Tuna's annual yard display contest is over and Helen Bedd and Inita Goodwin have broken Vera Carp's strangle hold on the trophy. But it seems they had some help from the Christmas Phantom who struck the Carp's yard in a big way.

THURSTON: *(Radio tape.)* He did.

ARLES: *(Radio tape.)* He did, he did. It seems when the judges arrived at the Carp's yard earlier this evening someone had put boxer shorts on the shepherds, the wise men and Joseph. And the Virgin Mary was wearing an ERA button.

(INITA exits to the kitchen.)

THURSTON: *(Radio tape.)* I was one of the judges and we laughed 'till our sides hurt.

ARLES: *(Radio tape.)* They did.

THURSTON: *(Radio tape.)* We did.

ARLES: *(Radio tape.)* They did, they did.

THURSTON: *(Radio tape.)* That's probably what stampeded those sheep.

(The TELEPHONE starts ringing. HELEN crosses to the radio.)

ARLES: *(Radio tape.)* They're still missing.

THURSTON: *(Radio tape.)* They are.

ARLES: *(Radio tape.)* But if anyone finds those sheep you can leave a message for Vera Carp at the clinic where she is recovering in the trauma unit.

THURSTON: *(Radio tape.)* Visiting hours just started.

ARLES: *(Radio tape.)* So go down there and get in line.

(HELEN turns off the radio, and crosses to answer the TELEPHONE.)

HELEN: Tastee Kreme, Helen speaking, how may I help you? ... Hello, Charlene. ... Hang on. ... Okay, shoot. *(HELEN writes on her imaginary pad.)* Uh huh. Uh huh. Uh huh. Uh huh. *(SHE chuckles on the last "Uh huh.")* That's one double cheeseburger with chili and the works, large fries, large D.P., large fried pie, one grilled cheese, grilled in margarine, not butter, trim the bread, hold the mayo and one diet D.P. You know, Joe Bob would be a lot less temperamental if he'd get off that diet. ... I am just trying to help. God, are you sensitive.

(SHE hangs up the phone and takes the order to the kitchen counter.) Inita, one wimpy cheese delight and one sweathog special with natural gas.

(We hear the sound of PLATES CRASHING from the kitchen. INITA appears at the counter.)

INITA: Oh, my God, Helen, we have a crisis.

HELEN: What now?

INITA: I was so nervous about the contest that I forgot to thaw the hamburger meat. If we have a big rush, Vernon will can me.

HELEN: Calm down. I've got my hairdryer back there in my bag. Use that to thaw it out.

INITA: Good idea. Where would I be without you?

HELEN: Unemployed. *(INITA disappears into the kitchen.)* And you'd better hurry up with that meat. Joe Bob's gonna have a fit if we're late with his supper.

(INITA re-enters.)

INITA: Joe Bob needs to take a powder.

HELEN: *(Getting an idea.)* And you know what? I've got some Painender P.M. out in my pick-up truck. I think I'll slip a couple in his diet D.P. just to calm him down.

INITA: Great idea. I'll watch the window. *(HELEN exits and changes to FARLEY. The TELEPHONE rings. INITA answers it.)* Tastee Kreme, Inita speaking, what can I do you for? ... Yes, Charlene, I'll remember to trim Joe Bob's bread. ... Yes, I'll remember to hold the mayo. ... Have I ever forgotten your large fried pie, Charlene? Goodbye.

(INITA hangs up. FARLEY BURKHALTER appears at the walk-up window. FARLEY is a Yosemite Sam type, "little person;" all that is visible is his head, hat and full bushy beard. [To achieve the short height, the actor walks on his knees on top of a 4-inch riser concealed behind the walk-up window.])

FARLEY: Hey, Inita.

INITA: Hi, Farley.

FARLEY: Congratulations.

INITA: Thank you. You comin' to the party?

FARLEY: We'd love to, but we're a little short on time. *(INITA laughs.)* What's so funny?

INITA: Nothin'. God, you little people are edgy. What can I do you for?

FARLEY: Give me two baby burgers and a medium fries.

INITA: You must be hungry today.

FARLEY: No, I got Phoebe out in the truck with me. We're gonna split the fries.

INITA: *(Looking out the window.)* Oh, yeah, there she is. I can just barely see the top of her head. She sure can rat that hair.

FARLEY: She wouldn't be four feet tall without it.

INITA: Hi, Phoebe. Merry Christmas.

FARLEY: She can't see ya, the seat's too low, but I'll tell her you said hi. How long will that food take?

INITA: I'll have it for you in a jiffy.

FARLEY: Thanks, you big old corn-fed thing, you.

(HE exits and changes to PETEY. INITA goes to open a sliding window in the "fourth wall.")

INITA: Julio, get off Helen's hood! Sit on your own hood, hood. Hector, you can't park there. You're not handicapped – yet. *(PETEY FISK appears at the walk-up window. Now in addition to his bandaged finger HE wears a neck brace, a wrist brace, and a bandage across his nose.)* Hi, Petey. I hope you didn't bring that coyote with you again.

PETEY: Fresno's only half coyote. And he hardly ever bites.

INITA: What can I do you for?

PETEY: I came by to see if you've got any left-over lettuce for Paula.

INITA: Oh, no, Petey. Look, Vernon don't want me throwin' anything away. If he finds out I'm giving left-over lettuce to a lizard, I'm in deep stuff.

PETEY: Paula isn't just any old lizard. She's a Mexican iguana with special dietary needs.

INITA: Iguana? Oh, God, Joe Bob Lipsey did a whole play about them once. Lots of nasty stuff about underwear salesmen. I hardly understood half of it.

PETEY: That sounds weird.

INITA: It was weird. This whole town thinks *you're* weird.

PETEY: Well, what'd you expect from a place that has an elk hunting season and no elk?

INITA: You're right there. There's not an elk within a thousand miles of here. *(INITA crosses to the kitchen counter.)* Look, Petey. I've got some romaine that's about gone. But I can't let you have the leaf lettuce. We're runnin' low.

PETEY: Thanks anyway, but Paula has a bad reaction to romaine. Last time I gave her romaine she bit me right between the eyes.

INITA: Get outta here, Petey, and take that four-legged handbag out there with you.

PETEY: Well, I never ...

(PETEY starts to leave, but INITA stops HIM.)

INITA: Well, alright, alright. Wait a minute. Here. Ain't nobody gonna be eatin' salads on Christmas Eve. *(SHE gives HIM the leaf lettuce.)* Merry Christmas.

PETEY: You, too, Inita. Paula says thanks.

(HE exits and changes to HELEN.)

INITA: Yeah ... Oh, God the meat!

(INITA runs off into the kitchen and changes to LEONARD. The TELEPHONE rings, but SHE ignores it. After the second ring, we hear the sound of a HAIRDRYER from the kitchen. On the third ring, HELEN enters and hears the phone.)

HELEN: *(To INITA who is offstage.)* Girl! *(Answering the telephone.)* Tastee Kreme, Helen speaking, how may I help you? ... Oh, hi. ... Hang on. *(Calling to the kitchen.)* Inita, flop one, cheesy greasy, let it bleed.

(INITA answers from offstage.)

INITA: *(Voice.)* Okee-dokee. Tell Aunt Pearl Merry Christmas.

Helen: *(Back into the phone.)* Mrs. Burras, Inita says

Merry Christmas. *(Towards the kitchen.)* You, too. *(Back into the phone.)* Do you want shaved ice or cube ice with that? ... Okay. Well, thank you. What a nice thing for you to say. Yes we're real proud that we won. I guess we really ought to thank the Phantom, though. ... Hello? Um, she hung on me.

(LEONARD CHILDERS, philandering gray-haired host of the Radio OKKK shopping program, enters at the walk-up window.)

LEONARD: Helen! Helen, have you seen my wife? Helen?

HELEN: Not yet, Leonard. But you know, that looks like her Land Rover pulling up right now.

LEONARD: Helen, I'd appreciate it if you'd not tell her you've seen me.

(HE exits and changes to JOE BOB.)

HELEN: You shoulda thought twice before you married a wilderness scout, Leonard. *(The TELEPHONE rings, HELEN goes to answer it, but as SHE does SHE is interrupted by the sound of a CAR speeding away, followed a moment later by a second CAR speeding away after the first. HELEN watches gleefully through the "fourth wall" window, then answers the phone.)* Tastee Kreme, Helen speaking, how may I help you? ... Yes, Charlene, I remember that was a large diet D.P. for Joe Bob. *(SHE puts the Painender P.M. into the drink.)* It'll be about ten minutes. ... We have a problem. ... I don't wanna get into it. ... Yes, I know Joe Bob is hypoglycemic. ... Listen, Charlene, you tell Joe Bob if he sets foot in Inita's kitchen he will be hypoglycemic with a limp. *(SHE hangs up.)* I hate this job.

(JOE BOB LIPSEY – director of the Tuna Little Theatre, grand, fey and constantly eating – enters.)

JOE BOB: Has Charlene called my order in?

HELEN: Oh, hi, Joe Bob. Inita, Joe Bob is here for his order.

(We hear a blast from the HAIRDRYER. JOE BOB shouts toward the kitchen.)

JOE BOB: I am hypoglycemic! I need food!

HELEN: Sit down, Joe Bob, you look weak.

JOE BOB: I haven't eaten for at least three and a half hours. I'm going in there to cook it myself.

(HE starts toward the kitchen. HELEN stops HIM.)

HELEN: That's a real bad idea, Joe Bob. Now sit down. Sit down. Here, have a big ol' jumbo Diet D.P.

JOE BOB: Thanks.

HELEN: Can I get you something to munch on while you wait?

JOE BOB: Anything! Peanuts! Bread crumbs! Dip a napkin in catsup; I need nutrition.

HELEN: Here, Joe Bob, you just munch on these chips, okay?

JOE BOB: That'll help. *(HE eats an imaginary chip, then spits it out.)* Oh, God. They're stale.

HELEN: Well I just serve 'em, I don't preserve 'em. *(SHE eats a chip and grimaces.)* Ummm. They are stale.

JOE BOB: Yeah, About as stale as this town. You have no

idea how I've suffered. I haven't had this many problems since that all-white production of *Raisin in the Sun.*

HELEN: Oh, I loved that one. It was so funny.

JOE BOB: An hour from now, I'm looking at an opening with a lead who can't find his teeth!

HELEN: How about a moonpie?

JOE BOB: Stanley Bumiller keeps slouching in the street scene like some thug.

HELEN: Big Hunk?

JOE BOB: The ghost of Christmas Past dips snuff and carries a spit cup. Inita keeps belching!

HELEN: Open wide for Chunky.

JOE BOB: And I asked the costumer for scarves. I get bandannas! I'm doing *Christmas Carol,* not *Rio Bravo. (HE rises and heads for the kitchen.)* I'm coming in there!

(HELEN lures HIM back to his chair with a pickled egg.)

HELEN: How about a pickled egg. Mm-mmm!

JOE BOB: I am bigger than this town.

HELEN: I heard that.

JOE BOB: Do you know what I am?

HELEN: What?

JOE BOB: I am a professional.

HELEN: Oh, yeah.

JOE BOB: I've been to Waco. I've worked the professional theatres from Corpus Christi to Flagstaff, and if Dixie Deberry thinks she's gonna cut off my lights, she can kiss my rosy pink butt.

HELEN: Ooooh. Inita, you need to get that food out here. I'm about to get sick. *(The TELEPHONE rings. HELEN goes to answer it.)* Tastee Kreme, Helen speaking. How may I help you? ... Yeah, but he's eating. ... Well, you know how he is when you get near his trough, ... Hang on. Joe Bob, it's for you. It's Charlene and she sounds real freaked out. Now you be nice to her.

(JOE BOB takes the phone.)

JOE BOB: What is it, fifth wheel? ... Charlene, I can't understand you, why are you crying? ... You're afraid of the dark? ... She what? ... She what?! That old horned frog cut off my lights.

HELEN: Oh, Joe Bob, I'm so sorry.

JOE BOB: It's alright, Helen. There's only one thing I want from this town before I leave.

HELEN: What?

JOE BOB: My grilled cheese sandwich, and I'm going right into that kitchen to get it!

(HE starts toward the kitchen. HELEN heads HIM off and THEY chase around the table.)

HELEN: Joe Bob! No!

JOE BOB: Out of my way, Helen.

HELEN: I can't let you do that.

JOE BOB: I'm coming in there, Big'un.

(JOE BOB exits into the kitchen.)

HELEN: Oh, no! Don't! Inita throws things! Oh, I hate this job.

(HELEN reacts as INITA and JOE BOB fight off stage.)

INITA: *(Voice.)* Joe Bob, get out of my kitchen!
JOE BOB: *(Voice.)* Out of my way, moose!
INITA: *(Voice.)* I'm warning you, Joe Bob.

(From the kitchen we hear the BONG of a frying pan hitting JOE BOB.)

JOE BOB: *(Voice.)* Ow! Oh! Damn! Oh!
INITA: *(Voice.)* Yeah! Now get out! And get yourself another street urchin.

(JOE BOB is thrown on stage. HE runs back off and we hear another BONG. JOE BOB staggers on stage.)

JOE BOB: Helen, will you do me a big favor?
HELEN: What?
JOE BOB: If I'm still in this town next Christmas, will you take me out somewhere and shoot me?
HELEN: Oh, Joe Bob. I couldn't do that. But I'll get one of my boyfriends to shoot you. They'd be glad to.
JOE BOB: I need a nap.

(JOE BOB exits and changes to INITA.)

HELEN: Yeah. Bye. Break a leg. Maybe I shouldn't have said that. Inita, are you alright?
INITA: *(Voice.)* Never better.

(Enter FARLEY's wife, PHOEBE, at the walk-up window.

SHE is a high-pitched "little person," and all that is visible is her tall hair, a prop wig manipulated by a stagehand.)

PHOEBE: Hey! Hey, Helen. Honey, get over here. How long is our food gonna be?

HELEN: It'll be just a sec, we had a small crisis.

PHOEBE: Hell, how long does it take you to cook two little baby burgers? What did you have to do, go out there and slaughter that steer?

HELEN: Listen, paperweight, we are having a bad day. Your food will be right out.

PHOEBE: I hope so. 'Cause we're just about to waste away out here.

(PHOEBE turns and exits. The TELEPHONE rings. HELEN answers it angrily.)

HELEN: Tastee Kreme, Helen speaking, how may I help you? *(HER tone suddenly turns sweet.)* Oh, hi, Randy. ... Oh, no, no trouble at all. All the time in the world. ... You what? You have a present? ... For me? Oh, you shouldn't have. ... Now? ... Oh, no, we're not too busy. But you better meet me out back, in case Vernon comes by. Boy, I'd hate to get canned on Christmas Eve. ... Ooooh, you, too. ... Ooooh, I'm heading that way. Bye. *(SHE hangs up.)* Inita? You gotta cover the front for a minute.

(INITA comes from the kitchen.)

INITA: Have you gone nuts? I'm up to my knockers in

frozen patties and now you just wanna rush off somewhere. There's no excuse for this, Helen.

HELEN: Yes, there is.

INITA: Like what?

HELEN: Randy.

INITA: Go for it, girl. *(HELEN exits and changes to GARLAND. The TELEPHONE rings. INITA answers it.)* Tastee Kreme, Inita speaking, what can I do you for? ... Look, Charlene, it's his own fault for coming into my kitchen. ... No, no, no, he started it. ... Charlene, get yourself a real man. We're all so tired of watching you bark up the wrong forest. *(SHE hangs up. A HORN honks out front. INITA yells out the walk-up window.)* Get off that horn, midget.

(GARLAND, the soda delivery man and one of INITA's boyfriends, appears at the walk-up window. GARLAND is tall and lanky, with a goofy, giggling laugh. [The actor achieves the extra height by walking on the same 4-inch riser that was used by FARLEY.])

GARLAND: Hey, Inita.

INITA: Oh, hi, Garland. Come on in and take a load off.

GARLAND: I'm on duty. I just came by to see if you need any more soda water.

INITA: We're fine, cute stuff. You know, Garland, I sure wish you came in cans. I'd pop your top every five minutes.

(GARLAND laughs.)

GARLAND: You crack me up, Inita. You know that?

INITA: What ever works. Garland, you could do me a big favor.

GARLAND: What's that?

INITA: Come 'round back to the kitchen and help me thaw out that hamburger meat.

GARLAND: Well, I'm on duty. ... Ah, I'll do you a favor just this once.

INITA: And I'll do you one later.

GARLAND: *(Laughing.)* You crack me up, Inita, you know that?

(HE exits and changes to HELEN. INITA calls after HIM through the window.)

INITA: Garland, use Helen's hair dryer to thaw that meat. *(GARLAND laughs again. The TELEPHONE rings and INITA answers it.)* Tastee Kreme, Inita speaking, what can I do you for? ... Oh, hi, Vernon. ... We're real busy, Vernon ... *(We hear the HAIRDRYER from offstage.)* ... Nobody's drying their hair at work. ... I don't know, clean out your ears. ... Tomorrow? What about tomorrow? ... Oh, no, Vernon. I'm not working on Christmas Day. ... Vernon, who's gonna eat out on Christmas Day? ... Your family? Oh, no. They can all go over to your house and fill up on baloney. ... You can't fire me, Vernon, 'cause I quit! And so does Helen. ... Well, why don't you kiss me where I can't reach?

(INITA hangs up. HELEN enters.)

HELEN: What is going on?

INITA: Helen, this is the worst Christmas of my life.

HELEN: What's wrong?

INITA: Vernon fired me!

HELEN: He what?

INITA: Well, actually I quit, 'cause he wanted to stay open on Christmas Day; and Kenny Ray is off in Fort Worth with my truck.

HELEN: Well, you can use my Mitsubishi anytime you want.

INITA: No, I can't. The last time Daddy caught me drivin' your Japanese truck, he boxed my ears. You know he fought in the Philippines. We couldn't even eat rice growin' up. Now I ain't got a job, no truck, no boyfriend.

HELEN: Well, you still have me and I'll work double shifts 'till you can get back on your feet.

INITA: Helen ...

(HELEN cuts HER off.)

HELEN: No, it's no problem. What are friends for. We'll have to cut back but we'll make it. And before long you'll be able to pay the back rent and over-due bills and for that stolen truck, and life will return to normal.

INITA: Helen ...

(HELEN cuts HER off again.)

HELEN: I don't want to hear it. As long as I've got a job, you've got a home. Just say that over and over in your mind. As long as Helen's got a job, I've got a home.

INITA: Helen.

HELEN: What?

INITA: You quit, too.

HELEN: I did?

INITA: Yes.

HELEN: Oh, no! Well, Inita, where are you gonna live?

*(INITA covers her face and cries as the lights fade and a
reprise of the honky tonk music swells. HELEN exits and
changes to PETEY; INITA exits and changes to R.R.)*

Act II, Scene 3-A

(We hear PETEY FISK calling from the distance.)

PETEY: Fresno! Fresno! *(PETEY enters to a stage that is
empty, save for the table and chairs. All around HIM is a vast,
starlit sky. PETEY is wearing the heavy bandaging as before,
and now also is using a crutch. HE is accompanied by his
imaginary pets: Paula the iguana, Fresno the coyote, and
VERA's runaway sheep. HE carries a small evergreen tree
with its roots in a burlap ball.)* Fresno, sit. Stay. Now, Fresno,
I know you're half coyote and you're not used to being
stampeded by hostile sheep. But if you bite me one more time
you're going to be making the call of the wild. And you sheep
stay over by the gate. Don't stampede the coyote. This natural
enemy thing is about to kill me. I'm down to my last arm and
leg. One more injury and we'll all starve to death. And Paula,
I know iguanas are prone to depression – but you're gonna
end up with a zipper and a snap if you don't lighten up. You
all ought to be ashamed of yourselves. Where's your
Christmas spirit? *(PETEY cautions the sheep.)* Hey, hey, stay
calm! Stay calm! Stay calm! Stay calm! ... Just stay calm. Let
me look for the star ... There it is. Fresno ... *(HE beckons to*

Fresno.) There it is, shining like the very first Christmas. We were all a part of it. Shepherds were watching their flocks of sheep by night – obviously there was a coyote problem – when they saw that star. And Joseph and Mary found no room at the inn, but the innkeeper said they could stay in the stable and that's where the baby was born, among the cattle and the sheep – and the iguanas. Look at it shine. You know, the light from that star left before there was even anybody here to see it. It's like looking at eternity. Shining down on everything. Peace on earth, good will to everybody. I never get tired of hearing that. Well, that's something to wish for. *(HE motions to his pets.)* Come on, now, Fresno. Paula, let's go inside. Girls, stay calm. We all need our rest. Tomorrow's Christmas Day.

(PETEY exits and changes to DIDI as the lights fade and music swells, a chorale of "HARK THE HERALD ANGELS SING.")

Act II, Scene 3-B

(The music fades out and lights fade up to a dim night scene. The stage is bare except for the table and chairs. We are in DIDI and R.R.'s yard. R.R. enters whistling 'WE WISH YOU A MERRY CHRISTMAS." As HE finishes the tune, HE hears an EERIE SOUND EFFECT. HE exits to investigate. DIDI enters wearing sunglasses and smoking her cigarette. SHE is pulling one end of a long, tangled orange electric extension cord. As SHE crosses, SHE sings a Christmas carol.)

Dɪᴅɪ:

OH, HOLY NIGHT, THE STARS SO BRIGHTLY SHINING.

IT IS THE ...

(SHE takes a drag from her cigarette, then picks up the tune right on beat.)

... BIRTH.

(At the other side of the stage SHE pulls out another cord and plugs the two together. The stage is illuminated from off stage by the blinding lights of her aluminum pan yard display tree. SHE steps back to admire it a moment, then continues singing.) Now that is one heavenly light!

FALL ON YOUR KNEES,

OH, HEAR THE ANGEL ...

(R.R. enters whistling "WE WISH YOU A MERRY CHRISTMAS." DIDI stops singing.) R.R., where in the hell have you been?

R.R.: Merry, Christmas, Didi.

Dɪᴅɪ: Is it? God-damn you, you did it again.

R.R.: You weren't supposed to peek at your Christmas present, Didi.

Dɪᴅɪ: Shut up. I have put up with your drinkin' ...

R.R.: I've been getting better ...

Dɪᴅɪ: And your tardiness ...

R.R.: I've been trying ...

Dɪᴅɪ: And your U.F.O. sightings ...

R.R.: I can't help it.

Dɪᴅɪ: And God knows the books never balance. But this Christmas is the topper, R.R. I have dropped hints for two months that all I wanted for Christmas was Sal Mineo's Greatest Hits and what do you give me? ... A Clue game!

R.R.: We can take it back ...

DIDI: We can't return it now. Mama's already swallowed half the pieces.

R.R.: Well, I'm sorry, Didi.

DIDI: *(Screaming.)* God-damn it. If I could have one Christmas wish it would be that one of your U.F.O.'s would pick you up tonight and haul your dead weight off to kingdom come! *(DIDI exits singing and changes to VERA.)*
FA LA LA LA LA, LA LA LA LA ...

(R.R. sighs. HE starts to whistle 'WE WISH YOU A MERRY CHRISTMAS" again. Three lines into the tune, a U.F.O. with massive lights and SOUND EFFECTS travels across stage above R.R. HE looks off stage and a high-tech, illuminated ramp lets down from the stage wing. R.R. looks in wonder, then exits up the ramp as the U.F.O. plays a huge, symphonic "... AND A HAPPY NEW YEAR." The ramp closes and the lights fade to black with only stars remaining as we hear the sound of the U.F.O. leaving. R.R. changes to PEARL.)

Act II, Scene 3-C

(Lights come up suddenly as VERA CARP enters riding in a motorized wheelchair. SHE is accompanied by a huge Christmas tree, which is so gigantic that the top disappears out of sight above the proscenium arch. SHE is speaking on the telephone.)

VERA: Hello, Sheriff, it's Vera Carp ... No, I'm not in the hospital anymore. Being around all those sick people depressed me so much I told the doctor to send a nurse home with me while I recover. Hold on ... *(SHE calls to offstage.)* Nurse? Nurse? Would you set that oxygen tent up over by the T.V.? ... Well! Well! *(SHE speaks back into the telephone.)* This nurse is such a grump. You'd think I'd asked her for a kidney. Most people would be grateful for the work on Christmas Eve – just my luck to bring home the Grinch. But back to business: I ran into Reba Childers over at the clinic. She was gettin' Leonard's bones set. Hold on ... *(SHE calls offstage in another direction.)* No, Lupe, alto! Alto! Lupe, you put that fur coat in the washer and I'll take back your Christmas bonus. *(Back into the telephone.)* Well, she understood that. Are you there? Where was I? Oh, right, Reba Childers. She examined the tracks around my yard display. She said there were two of them that did it. Females. Old. Old females, older than Egypt. One of 'em had combat boots and the other was a big old lady with a definite limp. Hang on ... *(To offstage.)* Virgil, put that down. Stop playing with that. That's not a toy boat, it's a bed pan.It won't float. Put the bed pan down now! *(Back to the SHERIFF on the telephone.)* Are you there? Well, what are you going to do? ... I don't want to hear it. ... Well, they should have thought about that. ... Well, ... Well, I suppose you're right. ... No, no, I wouldn't want anybody to go to jail on Christmas Eve. But come New Year's I want those two old dinosaurs singing "Auld Lang Syne" in handcuffs. Hold on ... *(SHE calls to offstage again.)* Virgil, put that down! Get that out of your mouth! That's not that kind of thermometer. *(To the SHERIFF on the phone.)* Let me call you back.

(VERA hangs up, quickly exits in her wheelchair and changes

to STANLEY. Her tree whisks away with HER and the lights fade.)

Act II, Scene 3-D

(We hear the end of an instrumental of "WHAT CHILD IS THIS?" as PEARL's Christmas tree glides into place. It is a traditional green tree with typically traditional ornaments. As the lights fade up, PEARL enters with an imaginary teapot. SHE pours into a cup on the table and puts the pot on an imaginary sideboard. SHE sits down at the table and begins licking stamps and sticking them on envelopes. SHE continues counting where SHE had left off before getting the pot.)

PEARL: One ninety-eight. *(SHE licks another.)* One ninety-nine. *(SHE spits – the stamps are getting distasteful – but licks another.)* Two hundred. *(SHE catches her breath and licks one more.)* Two hundred and one.

(SHE is exhausted. STANLEY enters.)

STANLEY: *(Dejectedly.)* Merry Christmas, Pearl.

PEARL: Oh, Stanley, come in. You're just in time for a Christmas toddy.

STANLEY: Oh, I've got plenty of time, Pearl. Dixie shut off the lights before I could finish my community service. You should see the smile on Rubber Sheets' face.

PEARL: *(Crossing to the sideboard to pour a toddy for STANLEY.)* Oh, Stanley, I've got tidings of great joy. I cut a deal with Dixie. She said you could lick stamps on next month's bills to finish your time and I just finished licking them for you. You're free to go.

STANLEY: Pearl, you didn't have to do that.

PEARL: Oh, I wanted to. I'm just glad we're a small town. One more stamp would have gagged me. And Stanley, lookey here, I've got something for you. It's a one-way ticket to Albuquerque, along with a little somethin' extra. You can thank your Uncle Henry for that spending money.

STANLEY: Pearl, why do you want me to go to Albuquerque?

PEARL: They say there's a lot of wildlife out there. You'll always have something to stuff.

STANLEY: Hell, Pearl, you think of everything. I wonder what Mama's gonna say.

PEARL: Now, don't worry about her. If Bertha ever needed to let something go, it's you. Now run along, That bus won't wait.

(STANLEY stands, toasts PEARL, and finishes his drink.)

STANLEY: I don't know how to thank you, Pearl.

PEARL: Just don't ever look back, Stanley, that's enough.

(STANLEY starts to exit but is afraid to go. HE moves to PEARL. PEARL takes STANLEY's hand. STANLEY kisses PEARL on the forehead.)

STANLEY: Bye, Pearl. *(There is a pause.)* Ain't you going to kiss me goodbye?

PEARL: No, I've licked too many stamps. I'm afraid I'd stick to you.

(STANLEY laughs as HE exits. HE changes to ARLES.)

    STANLEY: Hell, Pearl, you're crazy.

(PEARL gets up and waves after STANLEY.)

    PEARL: Oh, don't you say that, Stanley. I'm not.

(After HE is gone, PEARL picks up STANLEY's empty cup. A quiet reprise of "WHAT CHILD IS THIS" begins as SHE turns to go, pausing to switch off the lights of her tree. PEARL exits and changes to BERTHA as the lights fade and the music swells. The Christmas tree glides off after HER.)

Act II, Scene 3-E

(As the music continues, the lights fade up as the aluminum Christmas tree moves on stage. We are again at Radio Station OKKK. The table and chairs are as before and the light is on in the radio. ARLES enters and crosses to the table. As HE sits, HE punches a button to switch off the music, picks up a piece of paper and begins an announcement.)

    ARLES: This is Arles Struvie on Radio OKKK in Tuna, Texas. We're gonna be goin' off the air early tonight so we can have our annual Christmas party here at the station. Ever'body is invited to come on by, drop in, as long as you don't bring your kids – 'cause we don't want any fruit punch poured down our transmitters like last year. *(HE puts down the paper, then continues.)* We'd like to take this time to thank our sponsors here at Radio OKKK. Clifford's Piano and Organ Shop over in Sand City. Clifford wants you to know it's never too late to get your hands on a good organ. So come by Clifford's, talk it over, and remember: at Clifford's they will hold your organ 'til Christmas. This is Radio Station OKKK in Tuna, Texas, signing off.

(ARLES switches off the transmitter, and the radio light goes out. We hear BERTHA's voice as SHE enters, carrying an imaginary Frito pie.)

BERTHA: Knock, knock.
ARLES: Well, come on in.
BERTHA: Well, am I the first one here?
ARLES: Yeah.
BERTHA: No matter how hard I try to make an entrance at a party, I'm always the first one through the door. I guess that's my destiny.

(A tree light sparks, startling BERTHA.)

ARLES: Well, at least you get to see all the appetizers and jello molds before folks eat 'em up.

(BERTHA places her pie on an imaginary buffet table; SHE looks over the imaginary foods.)

BERTHA: Oh, there's a fancy one. *(SHE peers closely at it.)* What did she use to make the hooves?

(SHE takes a little taste, then picks up a buffet plate and begins dishing up food. ARLES takes an imaginary record off a turntable, puts it away in its sleeve and returns it to a shelf. HE looks around and glances at his watch.)

ARLES: I kinda wonder where ever'body is.

BERTHA: Well, I know Didi said she wasn't comin' because the party clashed with her T.V. schedule. She won't miss "Gunsmoke."

ARLES: And Thurston went over to Sand City. Woolco had a special on bubble lights.

BERTHA: *(Still adding food to her plate.)* I guess Leonard's still at the clinic.

ARLES: Oh, none of us have seen Leonard since Didi told the world about him goin' bowling with that red-headed bank clerk. We hear ol' Reba tracked him as far as Amarillo.

BERTHA: Amarillo?

ARLES: Oh, Reba can track a flea over concrete.

(BERTHA crosses to the punch bowl; ARLES counters.)

BERTHA: And she's a good shot when she finds what she's trackin', too.

(ARLES samples one of the hors d'oeuvres as BERTHA pours herself a cup of punch.)

ARLES: Deadly aim.

(ARLES grimaces at the taste of the food and puts it back.)

BERTHA: Well, I guess we shouldn't expect either one of them.

(BERTHA crosses to the table and sits. ARLES crosses to the punch bowl and pours himself a cup to wash away the bad taste.)

ARLES: So, is your husband coming by?

BERTHA: I haven't even seen him today. Hank's not very good at parties. Besides he never was one for Christmas. Some of my worst memories of Hank are of Christmas.

ARLES: *(Crossing to the table.)* You know, ol' Trudy could be the same way. She'd get meaner than hell right around Pearl Harbor Day and it could go all the way to Saint Patty's.

BERTHA: How long were you and Trudy married?

ARLES: Fourteen years.

BERTHA: That's a long time.

ARLES: Seemed like fifty. If we're gonna talk about Trudy I gotta have a snort. *(HE takes out his flask and pours into his cup. HE offers some to Bertha.)* You want some?

BERTHA: Oh, no. Thank you.

ARLES: Just a little snort in the punch?

BERTHA: No. It's against my religion.

ARLES: Well, who's gonna tell on ya?

BERTHA: I really couldn't.

ARLES: Well, if you really don't want any ...

(BERTHA cuts HIM off.)

BERTHA: Well, maybe just one little shot in my punch. That's Maxie Bovine's punch. I recognize that.

(ARLES pours, then sits.)

ARLES: Um. Bitter.

(BERTHA drinks.)

BERTHA: Mm, that's much better. What were we talking about?

ARLES: How awful Christmas can be.

BERTHA: Oh, my. It used to be terrible when the kids were little. Hank would get drunk and put all the toys together the wrong way. Then he'd get mad and disappear. But the worst Christmas ever was the year Hank got out of prison and didn't bother to tell anybody. I spent all Christmas Eve on a bus to Huntsville and him not even there. Turnin' around comin' home on Christmas Day with nine-year-old twins fighting every inch of the way, and Jody was just a baby. And Lord, was it cold. Everybody had colds, the whole bus was hackin'. Then at a rest stop in Big Spring Stanley talked Charlene into climbing into an empty luggage compartment. He locked her in and she screamed blue murder for ten solid minutes 'till I could find the bus driver to let her out. I'd have whipped them both had it not been Christmas. And it was cold.

(BERTHA finishes her punch. ARLES crosses to the punch bowl, taking BERTHA's cup.)

ARLES: Well, the worst Christmas I can remember was the year Trudy got mad and moved the trailer house one day while I was at work.

BERTHA: Why?

ARLES: Oh, hell, she was mad. She wanted an archery set for Christmas and I told her no.

(ARLES refills the cups.)

BERTHA: Why did she want an archery set?

ARLES: I have no idea. Hell, our insurance was high enough because of her driving. I wasn't about to give her a bow and arrow.

Bertha: And she moved the trailer?

ARLES: She moved it to New Mexico. *(ARLES crosses back to the table, handing BERTHA her cup on the way.)* Just flat out ruined my Christmas.

BERTHA: I can imagine. Having your home disappear across state lines like that.

(ARLES pours a shot into his punch, then offers BERTHA one.)

ARLES: You want another snort?

BERTHA: No, no, thank you.

ARLES: Just a little whiff in your punch?

BERTHA: I couldn't.

ARLES: A little dab'l do ya.

BERTHA: I mustn't.

ARLES: Well, if you really don't want any ...

BERTHA: Well, just one more little shot. *(HE pours just a little.)* A little bigger than that. *(HE pours HER a healthier shot, to overflowing.)* Oh, Arles!

ARLES: *(Pouring another for himself.)* And one for yours truly.

BERTHA: *(Becoming light-headed.)* Well, it's a shame nobody else showed up for this party.

ARLES: It is, it is. I was hoping to get a little dancin' in.

BERTHA: Dancing? I didn't know there was gonna be any dancing. I probably shouldn't even be here. In my church we don't dance.

ARLES: You want another snort?

(BERTHA puts her glass forward.)

BERTHA: Why not? *(ARLES pours a large shot for HER.)* You know one time in high school Vera and I sneaked over to Sand City and went to a dance. I let that slip one Saturday morning while Mama and I were cleaning the house and she whipped me with a vacuum cleaner hose.

ARLES: God almighty!

BERTHA: Mama had a way of breakin' your bad habits. Every time I shampoo rugs I think about that time. And I've never been dancing since. I don't even remember how.

ARLES: *(Rises, tipsy.)* Well, I'll show you.

BERTHA: Oh, hush. I'm Baptist.

ARLES: *(Heading back to the punch bowl.)* Well, I am, too. But you know what? When I go out of town on business or conventions or stuff I tell folks I'm a Methodist and I have one hell of a good time.

BERTHA: *(Presenting her empty cup to ARLES.)* You are lying.

ARLES: *(Refilling the cups.)* No. One time we raised so much hell in Houston I claimed to be an Episcopalian.

BERTHA: What was that like?

ARLES: I don't remember too much about it. By the time I came to I was back in Tuna feelin' like a Baptist again.

(ARLES hands BERTHA her filled cup.)

BERTHA: Episcopalian. Oh, my. I wouldn't have the nerve to do that, even for one night. Oh, Arles, it must be something, being a celebrity like you. You must have a lot of women after you.

ARLES: You'd think so, wouldn't you? *(HE crosses to sit again.)* But the truth is ever since ol' Trudy and I split the sheets I've kept every Saturday night open, but I always wind up playing Risk with Thurston or going over to Sand City with him for Chinese food.

BERTHA: No. A well-known broadcaster like you?

ARLES: It doesn't figure, does it? You know, I think the glare of the spotlights scares a lot of women off. And then Trudy said some mean things after the divorce, especially when the judge awarded me the trailer house. But hell, that trailer has been in my family for years.

BERTHA: It's practically an heirloom. The whole town knows that.

ARLES: But on the other hand, look at you, Bertha. *(THEY are BOTH getting a little drunk now.)* I mean, sure, you've got your kids. But Hank? God Almighty! It makes me mad as hell to think that that worthless husband of yours has had a loyal, well-fed gal like you waiting at home for him all these years and he never took you dancing, not once.

BERTHA: I told you, Arles, we're Baptist.

ARLES: I don't care. Even Baptists oughta sin once in a while. That's what church is for. It's a place you go to feel better after you've done some sinning. It oughta make you mad as hell that man never took you dancing.

BERTHA: It's beginning to the more I think about it.

ARLES: You want another snort?
BERTHA: Pour.

(BERTHA puts out her glass and ARLES pours a drink. HE swigs from the flask.)

ARLES: *(After a moment.)* If I was Hank, I'd take you dancin' twice a week.

(BERTHA knocks her drink over on the table. SHE is flustered as SHE dabs the spill with an imaginary napkin.)

BERTHA: Oh, Arles, I've spilled my drink. I really need to go now. I ...
ARLES: Stop. Don't budge an inch.
BERTHA: What?
ARLES: It's the way them radio tube lights bounce off your bouffant.
BERTHA: My hair? Is there tinsel in my hair?
ARLES: Shhh.

(ARLES moves to an imaginary stereo, picks out an album, places it on the turntable and carefully puts on the needle. Music starts to play, a slow, romantic instrumental. ARLES hitches up his pants. BERTHA, seeing this, gets up to go.)

BERTHA: Arles. I'd better be goin' home now ...
ARLES: Bertha, may I have this dance?
BERTHA: Well, Arles, I ... I don't ... *(A pause.)* Well, why not? I always wondered what it felt like to be a Methodist.

*(BERTHA crosses to ARLES and THEY timidly start to circle
slowly, not touching at first. ARLES puts his hands on
BERTHA's waist. THEY stop in profile and ARLES
indicates with his head for BERTHA to put her hands on
his shoulders. Finally, ARLES snuggles his head to
BERTHA's breast. THEY begin to dance, and when
BERTHA's back is turned to the audience, ARLES lets his
hands drop to BERTHA's rear end. HE slowly turns HER
around and we see her eyes grow wide as the music swells
and the lights fade. Just before the stage is black, the tree
lights spark once again.)*

THE END

*(Upbeat country Christmas music bumps in loudly for bows.
[NOTE: In the original production, all the Christmas
trees were also given a curtain call.])*

COSTUME PLOT

ARLES:

Act I:

Western yolk shirt *(no fringe)*, Dark green pants, Brown belt with small gold buckle, Casual loafer shoes, White socks, Straw cowboy hat *("Fort Worth pinch")*, Mustache.

Act II:

(Act I pants & belt, hat, mustache, socks), Fringed western yolk shirt, Light brown cowboy boots, Santa hat fitted over crown of hat.

DIDI:

Clear plastic raincoat with red raindrop print, lined with camouflage print, patched with multi-colored gaff and electrical tape, Clear plastic head bonnet lined with camouflage print, with frizzy dark hair at front and back, White ankle socks, Slip on "wedgie" sandals, Dark glasses *(added Act II, Scene 3-B)*.

PETEY:

Dark green pants *(same as ARLES)*, Waist-long blue denim coat, rigged to close askew, Dark gray cap with ear flaps, rigged with Velcro patch at front, 4x6 cards rigged with Velcro to attach to cap, imprinted with slogans: *SAVE THE WHALES, SAVE THE DOLPHINS, SAVE THE FIRE ANTS, SAVE THE DEER TICKS, SAVE THE SCORPIONS, SAVE THE LEMMINGS*, White socks *(same as ARLES)*, Loafer style shoes *(same as ARLES)*, Large, removable finger cast *(added Act I, Scene 3)*, Xshape bandage across nose *(added Act II, Scene 2)*, Neck brace *(added Act II, Scene 2)*, Wrist bandage (*added Act II, Scene 2)*, Crutch *(added Act II, Scene 3-A)*.

JODY:

Orange baseball cap, Striped T-shirt, Cut-off overalls, Tube socks, Short cut "little boy" cowboy boots.

CHARLENE:

Page-boy dark blond wig, Pink hair clips, Large lens glasses, Large lens pink sunglasses *(preset in her bag)*, Pink "A Chorus Line" T-shirt, Pink sweat shirt, Blue jeans with hip and butt padding, Pink bandanna strung through pants loops, Pink bandanna tied around one leg, Canvas shoulder bag with strap, Pink/white athletic shoes, White socks *(same as ARLES)*.

STANLEY:

Yellow sleeveless T-shirt, "Texas Taxidermy" logo, Faded blue plaid flannel vest *(shirt with arms cut off)*, Old blue jeans, Black "biker" boots with pants tucked in, Black bandanna tied around one leg, just above boot, Fake tattoo on upper right arm, Old jeans jacket *(Act II, Scene 3-C)*.

VERA:

Act I:

Peach-colored satin slip with bra, Peach-colored satin house coat, open at front with peach marabou feather trim, Blond wig, White "cat eye" glasses, Earrings, Knee-high hose, Peach sandals with marabou feather accent, White full-length "fake fur" coat, lined.

Act II:
Same as Act I, but in wheelchair, Peach "fake fur" lap blanket, No house coat.

DIXIE:
Grey, tight-curled wig, Large glasses with magnifier lenses, Knee-high hose *(VERA)*, Burgundy suit *(dress & jacket)*, Bright colored print blouse *(rigged into jacket)*, Big "army" boots, brown, Brown purse, with "$" forming handle.

HELEN:
Black wig, styled up, with small, white waitress cap, Purple bow on back of wig, Christmas earrings, False eyelashes *(removed after Act II, Scene 1)*, Elastic girdle with hip padding, Yellow uniform dress with breast padding and name tag, Hankie, White waitress apron, embroidered "Tastee Kreme", Panty hose, Clear acrylic high-heel sandals *(Frederick's of Hollywood)*, Burgundy fringed leather jacket, Small purple handbag.

FARLEY:
(Half costume only) Large straw hat rigged with full beard & mustache *(PETEY's denim jacket)*.

GARLAND:
(Half costume only) Khaki uniform shirt, embroidered with name and "soda" logo, Cloth wide-brim hat with band of bottle caps.

THURSTON:

Round tortoise shell glasses, Red/black plaid flannel shirt, Faded denim bib overalls; in bib pocket is a variety of pencils tipped with Christmas figures, Flesh hose, Black shoes, Santa hat.

ELMER:

Added to THURSTON: Black "gimme" hat with "NRA" patch, Dark blue windbreaker, rigged with quilted dark blue vest.

BERTHA:

Dark brown bouffant-styled wig, Poinsettia earrings, Large glasses with neck chain, Poinsettia print long-sleeve blouse, Kelly green polyester pants with matching vest, Christmas corsage, Red house slippers, Later add: Bright red flats, Large brown purse.

R.R.:

Full coveralls, Madras plaid jacket, Plaid bow tie, Small straw hat with madras plaid band, White rabbit's foot attached to coverall's zipper pull, Slip-on mesh shoes.

PEARL:

Act I:

Long blue flower print belted dress *(old-lady type)* with low-slung breast padding & butt padding, Pearls, rigged to dress, Black orthopedic shoes *(old-lady shoes)*, Flesh hose, Hat with Christmas decoration, Pearl cluster earrings, White gloves, Cane, Black purse.

Act II:
Full-length chenille robe with dickey, Red plaid booties, Mesh night cap, Cane.

SHERIFF:
(Half costume only) Light brown uniform shirt with Sheriff patches, Stomach padding, Silver Sheriff's star badge, Brown felt western hat with gold braid band, Mirrored aviator glasses.

IKE:
(Half costume only) Orange day-glow roadworker's vest labeled with "IKE" lettered in reflector tape, Orange day-glow hard hat with "IKE" lettered in mylar tape, Mustache, Long side-burns, Aviator dark glasses.

INITA:
Red wig styled up with waitress cap, False eyelashes *(removed after Act II, Scene 1),* Christmas earrings, Yellow uniform dress with bra padding and name tag, Hankie, White waitress apron embroidered "Tastee Kreme", Panty hose, White short socks, White athletic shoes, Red satin "Pro Rodeo" jacket, Small multi-color handbag.

LEONARD:
(Half costume only) Gray wig, Gray mustache, Blue western yolk suit jacket, White shirt, Bolo tie.

JOE BOB:

Magenta sun glasses, Gold neck chain, Stomach padding, Light beige safari suit *(jacket & pants)*, Bright tropical print shirt rigged into jacket, White short socks, Brown clogs.

PHOEBE:

(Prop only) Light brown wig styled very high *(Marge Simpson look)*, Three small bows on front, arranged vertically *(Wig mounted on wig head for operating)*.

PROPERTY PLOT

FURNITURE:
  Kitchen table *(Formica and chrome)*
  2 Kitchen chairs *(vinyl and chrome)*
  2 Old fashioned cabinet floor model radios
  Rolling palette with ornate peach upholstered arm chair,
      matching ottoman and VERA's shoes
  Rolling counter unit
  Motorized wheelchair with flowers attached to back
  2 Single step units *(used offstage)*

CHRISTMAS TREES:
  Radio Station OKKK: aluminum tree
      strung with practical lights and small pyro charges
      2 Christmas packages underneath
  Bumillers' house: scruffy green tree
      strung with practical lights
      2 Christmas packages underneath
      "STANLEY" license plate ornament
      (no star or ornaments)
  Didi's gunshop: green tree
      strung with practical lights
      decorated with hand grenades, shell casings, guns,
          and other instruments of violence
      gas mask with Santa hat as tree top ornament
      several Christmas packages underneath
  Tastee Kreme: fashioned out of tumbleweeds
      strung with practical chili pepper lights
      decorated with cowboy and western ornaments
      several Christmas packages underneath

Petey Fisk's: small evergreen tree
    base wrapped in burlap
Vera Carp's: gigantic green tree
    strung with practical lights
    decorated with gaudy, oversized ornaments
    many Christmas packages underneath
Aunt Pearl's: traditional green tree
    strung with practical lights
    decorated with traditional ornaments
    several Christmas packages underneath

U.F.O. & RAMP:
Practical light effect travels across stage
High-tech, illuminated ramp lowers from wing

HAND PROPS: *(all hand props are mimed except:)*
Ornament box containing:

> *Act I, Scene 2:* Crude, hand made angel, weighted clump of icicles, loose icicles, candy canes, a few other assorted traditional ornaments
> *Act I, Scene 3 add:* Hand grenade ornament, gun-in-holster ornament, 2 shotgun shell box ornaments, handcuffs ornament

Hand grenade ornament *(preset offstage),*Phoebe's hair *(see Costume Plot),*Long orange extension cord, in two lengths which plug together on stage, added to Bumillers' tree for bows: tinsel garland, star ornament, Christmas package.

LIVE SOUND EFFECTS PROPS:
Box of loose empty bullet shells, cowbell, hairdryer

Laugh-filled comedies from Jerry Mayer

ALMOST PERFECT

Buddy Apple's hilarious peccadilloes unwind in a laugh-filled comedy about marriage, adultery, career choices, a domineering father and finding one's identity. "Shrieking with laughter ... the audience knew exactly what Mayer was talking about."—*The Outlook.* "Winged one-liners and sitcom-styled 'takes.'"—*Los Angeles Times.* 3 m., 3 f. (#3130)

ASPIRIN AND ELEPHANTS

During a cruise from Copenhagen to St. Petersburg, three marriages change unpredictably in a rib-tickling romantic comedy that enjoys record-breaking runs in theatre after theatre. "Sails on a sea of comedy."—*Los Angeles Times.* "A sure-fire audience pleaser in the Neil Simon mode."—*Drama-Logue.* 3 m., 3 f. (#3587)

KILLJOY

In this unpredictable comedy/thriller Carol is tormented by her ex-husband and his new wife as they employ every trick in the book to put an end to paying alimony. "Jerry Mayer has been having hit after hit focusing on the humor and drama of marriage."—*Variety.* "Slays with laughs in a tight tale of deception and torment."—*Outlook.* 3 m., 3 f. (#13609)

A LOVE AFFAIR

This award-winning romantic comedy is brimming with hilarious as well as moving moments captured from a 38-year-long marriage. "Terrific."—*Hollywood Reporter.* "Warm of heart, quick of wit."—*Variety.* "Mayer keeps the humor constant."—*L.A. Magazine.* 2 m., 3 f. (#14937)

CAUGHT IN THE NET
Ray Cooney

This sequel to *Run for Your Wife* finds the bigamist taxi driver still keeping two families in different parts of London, both blissfully unaware of the other. However, his teenage children, a girl from one family and a boy from the other, have met on the Internet and want to meet in person since they have so much in common—name, surname and taxi-driving dad! The situation spirals out of control as John juggles outrageously with the truth. "A master class in the art of farce.... A precession-built laughter machine."—*What's On.* "Brilliant.... The funniest play of the year."—*Daily Mail.* 4 m., 3 f. (#5865)

THE UNDERPANTS
Carl Sternheim / Adapted by Steve Martin

The renowned actor and author of *Picasso at the Lapin Agile* provides a wild satire based on the classic German comedy about Louise and Theo Markes, whose conservative existence is shattered when her bloomers fall down in public. She pulls them up quickly, but he fears the incident will cost him his government job. Louise's momentary display does not result in scandal but it does attract two infatuated men, each of whom wants to rent the Markes' spare room. Oblivious of their amorous objectives, Theo happily collects rent from both the foppish poet and the constantly whining hypochondriac. "Funny stuff ... a fine play ... with lightning flashes of wit."—*TheaterMania.com.* 5 m., 2 f. (#23042)

For more plays by Ray Cooney, Steve Martin
and other masters of comedy, see
THE BASIC CATALOGUE OF PLAYS AND MUSICALS
online at www.samuelfrench.com

OSCAR AND FELIX
Neil Simon

America's comic mastermind has updated his classic comedy *The Odd Couple*, setting the trials and tribulations of Felix Unger and Oscar Madison in the present day. Those who love the original version as well as new audiences will laugh until they cry at this modern-day comic *tour de force*. Producers of *The Odd Couple*, the female version of *The Odd Couple* and *Oscar and Felix* are guaranteed a gleeful full house. 6 m., 2 f. (#822)

THE
INCOMPARABLE LOULOU
Ron Clark

The title character is a singer about to try for a comeback in a Staten Island nightclub. Meanwhile, LouLou's sister pushes her to publish her memoirs. The first performance is a bomb, but some of the sting is alleviated by the surprise appearance of an ex-husband who is now an up-and-coming congressman. Unfortunately, his attempt at reconciliation is only an effort to stop her from publishing certain incriminating photographs in her memoirs. "Delightful.... A confection that is irresistible."—*Miami News.* "A mine field of jokes and gags.... LouLou is pretty and delightful, vulnerable yet strong and beautiful in the way of a woman born with a natural sensuality."—*The Miami Herald.* 4 m., 3 f. (#10979)

For more plays by Neil Simon, Ron Clark
and other masters of comedy, see
THE BASIC CATALOGUE OF PLAYS AND MUSICALS
online at www.samuelfrench.com

ADULT ENTERTAINMENT
Elaine May

There is a cloud over porn queen Heidi the Ho's cable TV show. Her guests are mourning the passing of their employer and mentor, a legendary porn film maker. Tired of working for others, this motley group of adult video veterans decides to write and shoot their own extravaganza, an art film. Script one doesn't live up to their expectations so they bring in a new writer, one who insists they read the classics to prepare for their roles. Unexpected light bulbs go off and hilarity escalates. "May's best work ... surprises us with humanity in the midst of the ridiculous.... It's the comedy of the year."—*New York Post*. "Only a frenzied comic mind could imagine ... this delight ... with its giddy, raunchy sense of humor."—*Show Business Weekly*. 3 m., 3 f. (#3835)

MAN IN THE FLYING LAWN CHAIR
Caroline Cromelin, Eric Nightengale, Monica Read, Kimberly Reiss, Troy W. Taber and Toby Wherry

This high-altitude comedy of errors is based on the true story of Larry Walters, a man who secured his place as a cult hero for weird daredevils everywhere by using surplus weather balloons to launch himself to 16,000 feet in an aluminum lawn chair—and lived to tell about it. Developed through improvisation at the 78th Street Theatre Lab, this winner of the Edinburgh Festival's Best of the Fringe was aired on the BBC. 2 m., 3 f. (#14804)

For the largest selection of theatre comedy in print, see
THE BASIC CATALOGUE OF PLAYS AND MUSICALS
online at www.samuelfrench.com

Communicating Doors
ALAN AYCKBOURN

"A real knockout.... This is a show to see."—*New York Post*

"An inventive diversion."—*The New York Times*

This intricate time-traveling comic thriller by the British master of farcical comedy delighted London and New York audiences. A London sex specialist from the future stumbles into a murder plot that sends her, compliments of a unique set of hotel doors, traveling back in time. She and two women who were murdered in 1998 and 1978 race back and forth in the past trying to rewrite history and prevent their own violent deaths. 3 m., 3 f. (#5301)

The Dinner Party
NEIL SIMON

"A blizzard of one-liners.... The audience can bank on some good laughs."—*New York Daily News*

"Hilarious but also dangerously serious."—*New York Post*

Here is a decidedly French dinner party served up in a chaotic mode that only a master of comedy could create. Five people are tossed together in the private dinning room of an elegant Parisian restaurant for an evening that will forever change their lives. Playful antics, sudden zaniness and masterful comic dialogue punctuate the unfolding mystery. 3 m., 3 f. (#388)

Our *Basic Catalogue of Plays and Musicals* lists other comedies by Alan Ayckbourne and Neil Simon.

**Send for your copy of the Samuel French
BASIC CATALOGUE OF PLAYS AND MUSICALS**

The Tale of the Allergist's Wife
CHARLES BUSCH

"A window-rattling comedy of mid-life malaise [with] wall-to-wall laughs."—*The New York Times*

"Charles Busch comes of age as a comic playwright of the first rank."—*New York Daily News*

This winner of the Outer Critics Circle John Gassner Award and long-running Broadway hit concerns the depressed wife of a philanthropic allergist whose spirits soar when an incredibly fascinating and worldly childhood friend appears on her doorstep. Lee the savior that infuses life becomes Lee the unwelcome and sinister guest in short order. 2 m., 3 f. (#5301)

The Graduate

Adapted for the stage by
TERRY JOHNSON

Based on the novel by **CHARLES WEBB** and the screenplay by **CLADER WILLINGHAM** and **BUCK HENRY**

"Fun.... Definitely gives off starlight."—*The New York Times*

"Delightful."—*USA Today*

A hit in the West End and a popular show on Broadway starring Kathleen Turner, *The Graduate* brings the quintessential movie hit of the sixties—one of the most popular films of all time—vividly to life on stage. A college student spends his first summer out of school in the arms of his father's best friend's wife. Meanwhile, he is falling in love with the man's daughter. 6 m., 5 f. (#9196)

Send for your copy of the Samuel French
BASIC CATALOGUE OF PLAYS AND MUSICALS